# The Chase for the Mystery Twister

"You mean the tornado lifted up this car and dropped it five miles away?" Joe asked. He stared at the white car in disbelief.

"With a tornado that strong, it could happen," Diana said.

"The question is," Frank added, "where is the tornado now?"

They listened to the wind howling around them. Joe looked off to the left when five cloud-to-ground lightning bolts struck at once, illuminating a tornado funnel more than a mile wide.

"It's shifting," Diana said. "The tornado's coming back this way. It's headed right for us. We've got to get out of here—fast!"

# The Hardy Boys Mystery Stories

# Available from MINSTREL Books

# THE HARDY BOYS®

## 149

# THE CHASE FOR THE MYSTERY TWISTER

## FRANKLIN W. DIXON

A MINSTREL® BOOK

Published by POCKET BOOKS
New York   London   Toronto   Sydney   Tokyo   Singapore

A MINSTREL PAPERBACK *Original*

A Minstrel Book published by
POCKET BOOKS, a division of Simon & Schuster Inc.
1230 Avenue of the Americas, New York, NY 10020

Copyright © 1998 by Simon & Schuster Inc.

Front cover illustration by John Youssi

Produced by Mega-Books, Inc.

ISBN: 0-671-00123-X

First Minstrel Books printing April 1998

10  9  8  7  6  5  4  3  2  1

Printed in the U.S.A.

# Contents

# THE CHASE FOR THE MYSTERY TWISTER

# 1 A Rough Ride to Twister Alley

"Whoa!" Joe Hardy shouted as the left wing of the twin-prop commuter plane dipped and the plane shuddered, battered by strong winds.

"It's just turbulence," Frank Hardy assured his younger brother, not looking up from his book.

Joe peered out the window at the gray blanket of clouds surrounding them. The six-foot, athletically built seventeen-year-old was usually fearless, but small planes combined with bad weather made him nervous.

"I thought we'd be flying on a big jet," he said, running his hand through his blond hair and shifting uncomfortably in his seat.

"I guess no big jets go to Tulip, Oklahoma," Frank responded, casually turning a page.

"You'll need to put your tray table up for

landing," a flight attendant told Frank. Still reading, Frank pushed the table into its closed, locked position.

Joe looked at his slightly taller, brown-haired brother in wonder. "Either you have nerves of steel, or that's the greatest book ever written."

"We're going to be meeting the author," Frank explained. "I'd like to able to understand half of what he's saying."

"*Debris Patterns of Midwest and Central Plains Windstorms*, by Lemar Jansen," Joe read aloud from the book cover. "I don't suppose that's on the best-seller list."

"Do you want to take a look?" Frank asked as the plane pitched back and forth in the wind.

"Right now, I couldn't make sense of a comic strip, let alone a college textbook," Joe said. He closed his eyes. "Let me know when we're on the ground."

"Now," Frank replied.

Joe's eyes snapped open just as the wheels touched down. A few seconds earlier, all he could see were gray clouds. Now the small plane was braking on the runway. He looked above at the dark, ominous sky. "Wow, that's what I call low cloud cover."

"Let's hope Phil is on time," Frank said, sliding his book into his carry-on bag. "I hope we can get off the road before those thunderclouds let loose."

* * *

The Tulip, Oklahoma, airport was so small, there was no baggage carousel. As Frank and Joe scanned the luggage lined up against a wall inside the terminal, they heard an announcement: "Frank and Joe Hardy, please report to the customer service representative in the baggage claim area."

The Hardys turned and began to laugh when they saw their friend Phil Cohen standing close by, speaking through his cupped hands. Beside him were their two suitcases.

"You are now looking at the customer service representative," Phil said. "Let's get a move on."

In the parking lot, Phil hefted his friends' suitcases into the bed of a battered 1973 blue pickup truck.

"These are your wheels?" Joe asked, nudging Frank.

"Hey, I'm just an intern," Phil replied. "I'm lucky Mr. Jansen lets me drive *any* of the Windstormers' vehicles."

"Windstormers?" Joe asked.

"That's the name of Mr. Jansen's tornado-chasing team," Frank told his brother.

Joe felt the dimpled depressions on the truck's roof and hood. "It looks like someone took a hammer to this thing."

"Any storm-chasing vehicle worth its salt has those," Phil said proudly. "They're from hailstorms that happen often around here."

Phil told his friends more about his spring internship with Lemar Jansen, one of the leading researchers and experts on tornado debris patterns. "I've had to learn a lot about meteorology—the study of weather—and how to operate the different equipment used to forecast and track windstorms."

"Sounds exciting," Frank said.

"It does, doesn't it?" Phil said. "So far, though, it's been a lot of hard work and waiting around. But I think that's about to change."

As they pulled out onto the two-lane highway, a hard rain began to fall. "Talk about a lousy day for traveling," Joe said.

"That's true, but it's a perfect day for the first tornado of the season," Phil noted, gazing up at the threatening sky. "Warm air has been pushed up from the Gulf of Mexico and moved beneath the cold, dry air left over from winter."

"If I understand Mr. Jansen's book correctly, that spells trouble," Frank concluded.

"It spells fun if you're a Windstormer," Phil replied.

"Cool. The only twister I've seen is the one that dropped Dorothy's house in Munchkinland," Joe said with a smile.

"Well, Joe, you've come to the right place to see the real thing. We're in Twister Alley," Phil said. He flipped the windshield wipers to full speed as the rain increased. "More tornadoes

4

touch down here than anywhere else in the world. In fact, some locals call the town of Lone Wolf the tornado capital of the world.''

"That's a distinction I'll bet they could live without. It must be really bad for tourism," Frank said.

"You'd be surprised, Frank," Phil replied. "Tornado chasing has become a thrill sport for a lot of people."

Joe spotted the headlights of a tractor-trailer coming toward them from the other direction.

"Sounds like a dangerous pastime," Frank remarked.

"Dangerous in a lot of ways," Phil agreed. "Mr. Jansen had a lot of close calls last tornado season. He and his researchers nearly collided a dozen times with thrill seekers following the same twister."

As the tractor-trailer drew closer, it sounded its horn loudly. "Phil—" Joe warned his friend.

The huge semi passed within a few feet of their pickup truck, creating a crosswind that drove the smaller vehicle off onto the soft shoulder of the road. Phil countered, keeping a firm grip on the steering wheel and turning back toward the highway.

Frank's head shot back as the passenger side of the truck passed within inches of a posted speed limit sign before Phil finally brought the pickup back onto the highway and under control.

"Man! That guy must have been doing ninety!" Joe exclaimed.

"I wonder where he's going in such a hurry," Frank said.

"The only thing in that direction is Tulip," Phil replied.

"We should report the driver before he really hurts someone," Frank suggested. "Did anyone get a look at what company owns the truck?"

"It was unmarked," Joe replied. "Just painted plain white. The guy inside had black curly hair and a mustache, but that's all I could see."

"Did you notice the Doppler effect?" Phil said out of the blue.

"The what?" Joe asked.

"The Doppler effect," Phil repeated. "As the truck got closer, the acoustic waves of his horn rose in pitch. After it passed, the sound faded to a dull moan."

"Phil, we were a few inches away from being roadkill back there," Joe said. "This is probably not the best time to be giving us a science lesson."

"Sorry," Phil said, smiling. "I've just learned so much from Mr. Jansen the last two weeks. It's the principle of how the Doppler radar works. That's what the Windstormers use to track tornadoes."

"I read about that," Frank told his friend. "A radar reflection from a moving object changes

6

frequency, depending on whether the object is moving toward or away from the radar."

"In our case, the moving object is the tornado," Phil added. "That's how meteorologists get the computerized images of storms that they show on the TV news."

"Well, right now the radar in my stomach is trying to bounce some waves off the nearest burger place," Joe joked.

"Good luck." Phil laughed. "There's nothing but cornfields for the next ten miles."

A garbled voice suddenly crackled over the citizen's band radio in the truck. "How close are you to Route Thirty-one, Greg? Come on?"

"Sounds like we picked up some trucker on your CB," Frank said.

"No, this is set to a special frequency," Phil replied as he turned up the volume.

"I see it, Jed. Looks like an F two," another garbled voice replied.

"Who is that?" Joe asked.

"Jed is Jed McPlat. Greg is his boss," Phil said, tilting his head to look at the sky through the top of the windshield.

"His boss? In what business?" Frank asked.

"The storm-chasing business," Phil replied. "Greg Glover and his team are our chief competition."

"Buckle your seat belt, Jed," Greg Glover's voice came over the radio.

"That sounded loud and clear. They must be getting closer," Frank said.

A split second later, a black truck mounted on giant tractor tires tore out of the cornfield to the right of the highway.

"Look out!" Frank shouted, bracing himself for the collision. "It's going to hit us!"

# 2 In the Shadow of a Twister

Phil spun the wheel to the left. The pickup truck skidded sideways, then fishtailed back again, barely missing hitting the monster truck head-on.

Phil angrily grabbed the CB microphone. "Greg Glover, this is Phil Cohen. Are you nuts?"

"Phil!" Joe shouted, grabbing the steering wheel and spinning it to the right. Another vehicle had emerged from the cornfield, and Joe's quick hands avoided a collision. Phil dropped the CB microphone and put both hands on the wheel.

A van, then another car, and another came tearing through the cornfield and crossed the rural highway in front of them, following Glover's monster truck. Phil swerved right, barely missing the rear bumper of the first car before stopping inches away from the second car as it whizzed past.

"We're safer in a cornfield than on that obstacle course," Phil shouted to his friends, hitting the gas and joining the pursuit.

"They're driving like they have the law after them," Joe noted.

"It's not what's after them, it's what they're after," Phil replied.

"I see it!" Frank shouted as the truck cleared the cornfield and bounced over the crest of a low hill. From the base of a great wall of dark clouds, a funnel cloud had formed, and as the boys watched, a thin tail stretched down hundreds of feet and made contact with the earth.

"A twister!" Joe said in wonder.

Immediately, the CB radio waves were jammed with excited voices pointing out what everyone already knew: the first tornado of the season had arrived.

Ahead, Joe saw Glover's monster truck dip down into a ditch and up the other bank. The giant tires gripped the solid ground beneath the muddy field beyond, spewing mud and water high into the air behind it.

The car behind Glover tried to follow, but its wheels got stuck in the muck. The other Glover vehicles stopped short on the near side of the ditch.

"No way, Phil," Joe warned.

10

"I know," Phil replied. He turned left onto a dirt road that ran parallel to the empty field.

Frank now had a good view of the twister through the passenger window. It crossed an open field, pulling an oil derrick from its mooring. Crude oil was sucked up into the gray whirlwind, turning it black.

"Come in, Wind Six," a low voice came over the radio.

"This is Wind Six," Phil responded.

"Tracking," the low voice continued, then paused. "The F two is turning southeast."

"Southeast?" Frank asked, looking behind them. "That's in the opposite direction!"

"Ignore it," Phil instructed, eyeing the black monster truck paralleling them on the other side of the ditch. "The guy in that truck is trying to mislead us."

The twister continued moving northwest, plucking the tin roof off a dilapidated barn. A few moments later, it flung the roof back to the ground in a twisted mess.

"Look, it's a fire engine!" Joe shouted, pointing toward one of several vehicles about a mile beyond the tornado.

"That's not a fire engine," Phil said with a grin. "It's Mr. Jansen!"

Frank realized that what Joe thought was a fire engine was in fact a red customized bus, with a number of radar dishes and antennas sticking out from every side.

11

"Jubjub, Bandersnatch!" another low voice radioed in.

"Snicker-snack, snicker-snack!" Phil replied into the CB microphone. Frank and Joe looked at each other, puzzled.

"It's code," Phil said, nodding toward the black monster truck across the ditch, "so that we don't fall for Greg Glover's false reports."

"Is that who the first voice was?" Joe asked.

"You guessed it," Phil replied. "Now I'm talking with Mr. Jansen."

"Doppler shows continued northwesterly movement," the low voice replied.

"Got it, Wind One," Phil replied. "I have friends in tow."

"Roger that, Wind Six," came the reply. "Back off to a safe distance. Do not attempt to intercept."

"Roger. Wind Six out," Phil said, replacing the microphone in its cradle and slowing down the truck. "Sorry, but Mr. Jansen wants us to give up the pursuit."

Joe frowned. "I was having fun. Too bad we couldn't have gotten a little closer to it."

"We may not have a choice. Look!" Frank said, pointing to a man in a broad-brimmed hat and overalls standing in a field in the path of the tornado. The man's hands were cupped around his mouth, as if he was shouting something.

"Why isn't he looking for cover?" Joe wondered aloud.

The man suddenly ran toward a lone oak tree and picked up something that was lying beneath it.

"Looks like he's got a big dog in his arms!" Frank shouted over the howling wind.

"I'll radio Mr. Jansen," Phil said.

"He'll never make it!" Joe shouted. "And Glover is ignoring the man. We're the only ones close enough to get to him before the twister does!"

Frank nodded his agreement. "There's a bridge across the ditch about a quarter of a mile ahead."

"Okay, guys," Phil said. "Hang on to your heads."

"You mean our hats?" Joe asked.

"If we only lose our hats, we'll be lucky!" Phil replied loudly as he turned off the dirt road and crossed the bridge into the gourd field beyond.

The man was running toward a farmhouse but was slowed by the weight of the dog he was carrying. The sound of the tornado grew deafening as they got closer. Frank thought it sounded like a thousand freight trains running through his head.

The blue pickup was at the outer edge of whirling debris surrounding the twister. The windshield was suddenly splattered in a deluge of black.

"It must be oil from the derrick it tore down!" Frank shouted.

13

Beside Frank, Joe nodded. But Phil, only a few feet away in the driver's seat, shook his head, unable to hear. The windshield wipers only spread the mess, and now they couldn't see at all.

Frank pointed to himself and then his window. After rolling it down, Frank kneeled on the seat and stuck his torso out the window. His vision was still obscured, but Frank could see enough to know they were off course and headed directly for the funnel of the storm.

"Turn left!" Frank shouted.

"Turn left!" Joe screamed into Phil's ear, relaying the message.

Frank caught sight of the man's silhouette through the dust-filled air.

"Stop!" Frank shouted at the top of his lungs.

Phil must have heard Frank, because he stomped his foot hard on the brakes, nearly tossing Frank out the window. Frank opened the door and ran to the man and his dog, leading them back to the truck. Joe took the hound dog and passed it on to Phil, while Frank pushed the man up onto the seat and then squeezed in behind him.

"I don't think this truck cab was made to fit four men and a dog," Joe said, his head pressed against the roof and his face squashed against the dog, which was licking Joe's cheek.

The farmer Frank had rescued looked to be about twenty and was tall and slim, with sandy blond hair and a pointed nose. "We have to make

14

it to the storm shelter beside my house!" the young farmer shouted as Phil stepped on the gas.

Joe looked through the back windshield. They were gaining a little ground on the whirling menace, which Joe felt was following their every move.

"Get ready to abandon ship!" Frank shouted, spotting the doors to the underground storm shelter.

As Phil brought the truck to a halt, they flung open the doors and made a run for the shelter. Joe grabbed the dog. The wind whipped the dust at such high speeds, it felt like hundreds of pins pricking Joe in the face.

Frank helped the farmer open the shelter door, beneath which was a set of stairs leading down fifteen feet to a storage area.

"Here, Joe!" Frank shouted, guiding his brother and the dog to the entrance and down the steps.

Once they were down, the farmer slammed and locked the door behind them. Immediately, the door shuddered from the impact of the tornado, which seemed to be passing within a few feet of them.

Frank and the young farmer held fast to the inside handles of the shelter door, pulling with all their might against the powerful updraft threatening to tear the door off its hinges.

The next twenty seconds lasted forever, Frank thought. Then the roar died to a low din, and the door stopped shaking. The farmer lit a lantern, revealing a room filled with canned foods and emergency supplies. Phil coughed up dust. Joe could barely open his eyes, they were so caked with dirt. The dog sneezed.

"Bless you, Bullet," the farmer said to his dog. He turned to Frank, Joe, and Phil. "I'm Snowdon Parlette. I don't know who you guys are, but me and my dog thank you."

"I'm Frank Hardy, and this is my brother, Joe," Frank said, looking for a clean part of his sleeve to wipe his face.

"I'm Phil Cohen," Phil said with a slight wheeze.

"I've seen you in town," Snowdon told Phil. "Hanging out with that storm-chaser guy."

Frank patted Bullet's head. "Maybe next time you'll know to come when your master calls you."

"Oh, he knows," Snowdon said, rubbing his dog's ear. "He just can't hear too well anymore. Can't see, neither. But his nose is just as keen as when he was a pup."

"Let's talk more outside," Joe suggested, starting up the steps.

"I wouldn't advise it," Snowdon warned. Suddenly, the door began to shake as the roaring wind returned. Startled, Joe stumbled back down the stairs.

"We were in the center of the funnel," Snowdon explained, once again gripping and tugging the door handle to keep the shelter sealed. The howling of the wind began to fade, and after another ten seconds, it was gone. "Now it's passed," Snowdon said.

They waited another five minutes to be sure, then emerged from the shelter.

Mr. Jansen's red bus and the other Windstormer vehicles were all around, and the team had already begun to record data.

Frank looked in every direction. The twister had vanished. "What happened to the tornado?" he asked Phil.

"It died out. Small ones don't usually last long," Phil said.

"Small ones?" Frank repeated in disbelief.

"Yeah, that was probably an F two," Phil explained, surveying the damage around them. "An F five is the biggest. The funnel can be more than three miles across."

"I'm sure glad we brought our heavy-duty suitcase," Joe said, walking away from his brother.

"Where are you going?" Frank asked.

"To get our luggage," Joe replied, pointing to their bags, which had been carried out of the back of the pickup and dropped in the field at least fifty yards away.

As Joe was returning with the suitcases, a man with a bass voice, a brown beard, and wearing glasses strolled over. "Are you all right, Phil?" he asked, seeming preoccupied with the clipboard on which he was feverishly writing.

"Fine, Mr. Jansen," Phil said, coughing again. "A little dusty."

Phil introduced Frank, Joe, and Snowdon.

"Welcome to Twister Alley," Jansen said.

"Thanks, we're glad to . . ." Joe began to reply, but Jansen had moved on, calling out instructions to another member of his team.

"Do you own this farm?" Frank asked Snowdon.

"I wish," Snowdon replied. "It's my dad's. But he's down in Dallas on business." Snowdon looked around at the damage caused by the tornado. "Boy, is he in for a surprise when he gets back."

The Parlette barn was lying upside down in the middle of an okra field. "I'm just glad that Dad was able to buy tornado insurance last month from good ol' Toby Gill," Snowdon added.

A young woman with long black hair, and wearing faded blue jeans and an untucked flannel shirt, walked up. "Phil, would you mind getting the video camera out of Wind Three?"

"My pleasure, Diana," Phil replied, then introduced Diana Lucas to his friends.

"So, Diana, how do you like Oklahoma Tech?" Frank asked.

"Fine," Diana replied, arching her eyebrows, curious.

"You're a senior majoring in physics," Frank continued.

"Yeah. How did you know? Are you a mind reader?" Diana wondered.

"No," Frank said, smiling. "I got all that from the college ring on your finger. The symbol for physics on one side, your class year on the other."

"Frank and Joe's dad is a private detective back in our hometown of Bayport, New York," Phil said to Diana.

"And you two are following in his footsteps?" Diana finished the thought.

"You could say that," Joe replied. "But right now, we're just here on spring break to visit Phil."

"Then welcome to Oklahoma," Diana said, gesturing to the destruction around them and smiling. She turned to Phil. "Let's get some videotape of the debris pattern starting at the property line and running to the overturned barn."

Phil nodded and headed off toward a dented gray off-road vehicle that the Hardys assumed was Wind Three.

"What do you mean by debris patterns?" Joe wondered.

"Can you see the track that the tornado took?" Diana asked, pointing and tracing the path the tornado had taken.

"Yeah," Joe replied. "It kind of looks like slightly overlapping letter *C*'s."

"Right. Notice where it deposited ninety-five

19

percent of all the junk that it tore up?" Diana asked him.

Joe hesitated, then realized. "To the left of the tornado's path!"

"Correct," Diana explained. "And that's how the debris pattern is every time. By studying it—"

"Not every time," a voice interrupted her. It was Lemar Jansen, who had overheard the conversation while passing by. "Five years ago, in New Mexico, I studied the aftermath of a twister that destroyed an isolated ranch house in the desert. The entire contents of the place had been hurled in every direction. I never have figured that one out."

"A mystery twister," Frank said.

"A mystery twister," Jansen repeated, looking at Frank closely. "I like that."

"I need to get into town to talk with Toby Gill, the insurance man," Snowdon said. "Why don't you and Joe come on in and clean up?" he said to Frank.

"Thanks," Frank replied, looking at their wet, muddy clothes. "I think we'll take you up on that."

As the Hardys followed Snowdon around the side of the farmhouse, Joe saw a strange, hairless creature scamper by, clucking.

"Looks like the tornado hit our hen house," Snowdon grumbled, pointing to the remains of a small wooden structure.

"That was a hen?" Joe asked. "What happened to all its feathers?"

"Plucked. That's what tornado winds can do," Snowdon replied as he opened the door to his blue pickup.

"I'm afraid the winds did more than defeather your chickens," Frank said, nodding toward some rusty nails that had pierced and flattened two of Snowdon's tires.

"Well, doesn't that just beat all," Snowdon said, shaking his head and throwing his hat on the ground.

"Maybe Phil can give you a ride into town," Joe suggested.

Just then Phil came running around the corner of the farmhouse, shouting with excitement. "Mr. Jansen got a phone call from Tulip. Another tornado just touched down. I need to assist him on the remote weather station," Phil added, referring to the red bus that had pulled around the house to pick him up.

"We'd better stay here and help Snowdon," Frank said. "Can we borrow the Blue Bomber?"

"Sure thing," Phil replied, tossing Frank the keys as he ran to board the bus.

The Hardys watched as the bus and four other vehicles sped up the dirt road leading from the Parlette farm and pulled out onto the highway, headed back toward Tulip.

"So much for small-town life being quiet," Joe said. "We've been here an hour, and we've already had more excitement than we've seen in Bayport all year!"

The town of Lone Wolf, Oklahoma, was indeed small, and it was ghostly, too, Joe thought. They drove by several ruins left by past tornadoes, including a crumbled brick house that had posted in front of it a hand-painted sign that read: Used to Be 125 Main Street.

A van from Channel 9 News, Lone Wolf, buzzed past them, headed back toward Tulip.

"There's Mr. Gill's place," Snowdon said, pointing to a small office tucked among the old-time storefronts along Main Street. Frank parked in front, and the Hardys and Snowdon entered the insurance office, the little bells on the door jingling behind them.

"Whoa," Joe said, looking around the small office. "It looks like a tornado hit in here, too."

The drawers of Gill's desk were hanging open, as were the drawers to his filing cabinet. Papers were strewn across the room, and a broken desk lamp lay on the floor.

"This couldn't be tornado damage," Snowdon said. "The doors were closed, and none of the windows is broken."

Frank heard a beeping noise and traced it to Gill's telephone, which was lying on the floor under the desk. Snowdon reached to hang it up. "Don't!" Frank warned. "We don't want to touch anything. We need to get fingerprints."

Joe found that the back door to the office had been left ajar and led to an alleyway. A man with gray-streaked long black hair was parked there in a green station wagon. Seeing Joe, the man burned rubber and sped off just as Frank and Snowdon stepped into the alley.

"Hey!" Joe shouted after him, then turned to Snowdon. "Was that Toby Gill?"

"No," Snowdon replied, wrinkling his forehead. "No, it wasn't." He turned and walked back inside without saying anything else. Joe and Frank exchanged a curious glance.

Back inside the office, Snowdon and the Hardys examined the mess, being sure not to touch anything.

On a shelf, Frank saw a framed photo of a man seated at a desk. He was blond and balding, with a small upturned nose and a friendly smile.

"That's Mr. Gill," Snowdon said.

"Do you know what was in here?" Joe asked, standing over a filing cabinet that had been completely emptied.

"That's where Mr. Gill kept all the insurance policies," Snowdon said. "I think—" Snowdon stopped midsentence. He reached down and picked up a small oblong object from the floor.

"Don't touch anything," Frank reminded him.

"It's just . . . my pocketknife," Snowdon replied, showing him the ivory-cased blade. "I must have dropped it."

"This looks like a break-in. We'd better contact the local police," Frank suggested.

"Hold it!" a voice behind them shouted.

Snowdon and the Hardys turned to find themselves facing a man in a white barber's jacket. The man stood in the doorway, holding a gun belt in one hand and a revolver in the other.

"You make one move, and I'll shoot you where you stand!" he commanded.

# 3 The Disappearance of Toby Gill

"Sheriff San Dimas?" Snowdon said. "It's me, Snowdon Parlette. Andrew Parlette's son."

"What are you doing in Toby's office?" the man in the barber's jacket asked.

"I came in to fill out some claim forms," Snowdon explained. "Dad's out of town, and our farm got hit hard by the twister that just came through."

"It looks like all the insurance files are missing," Frank said.

"Who are you?" the sheriff asked.

"Frank Hardy. And this is my brother, Joe," Frank replied.

"They're friends with Mr. Jansen and his group, Sheriff," Snowdon added.

"*Buenos días.* I'm Carlos San Dimas," the

sheriff said with a nod. "Old Mr. Wilkie came in here to see Toby a few minutes ago," San Dimas explained, lowering his revolver. "He fetched me from the barbershop. Said Toby Gill's place had been ransacked."

"I'm confused, Mr. San Dimas," Joe said. "Are you a barber or the sheriff?"

"Both," San Dimas replied, putting his revolver back in the holster of the gun belt. "Lone Wolf doesn't have enough crime or enough money to hire a full-time sheriff. So when I'm not fighting crime, I'm cutting hair."

San Dimas walked over to the open filing cabinet. "Did you boys touch anything?"

"No, sir," Frank said. "Our dad is a retired detective, so we're pretty familiar with police procedure."

San Dimas nodded with satisfaction. "And you saw no sign of Toby?" he asked.

The boys shook their heads.

"When's the last time anyone's seen Mr. Gill?" Joe wondered.

"I saw Toby opening up his office at six this morning. He smiled and waved at me," San Dimas replied, kneeling beside the phone.

"The phone was off the hook when we got here," Joe told him.

The sheriff picked up the receiver with a clean handkerchief and hung it up. The loud, piercing beep was silenced. "Anything else you can tell me?"

"No," Snowdon replied quickly.

"Actually, yes. There's one thing," Joe said, correcting him. "In the alley, I saw a man in a green station wagon drive away the second he saw me."

"A green station wagon?" San Dimas repeated, turning to look Snowdon in the eye. "Did he have long black hair? An older man?"

Snowdon didn't answer, so Frank spoke up. "Yes, sir. But Snowdon said it wasn't Toby Gill."

"No, it was Henry Low River," San Dimas told them. "He's a woodcarver. Lives in Tahlequah, a town in the Cherokee Nation."

"So?" Snowdon said, bristling. "He was driving down the alley. What does that mean?"

"It means I'd like to talk to him about Toby's disappearance," San Dimas replied.

"Disappearance?" Snowdon shot back. "Who's to say that Mr. Gill didn't have to leave to take care of some emergency?"

"Look at this ransacked office, Snowdon," San Dimas replied. "Henry Low River has held a grudge against Toby for more than a year. He's threatened him repeatedly."

"Henry's threats were just a lot of talk," Snowdon insisted. "He would never harm anyone."

"Mr. Low River is a strange character. I'm not so convinced he's harmless," San Dimas replied. "Now, unless you have any more information to

27

give me, I'm going to ask you boys to leave the premises. I'm declaring this office a possible crime scene."

After giving the sheriff information on where they could be reached, Frank, Joe, and Snowdon climbed into the truck and headed back toward the Parlette farm.

"Looks like our friendly visit may be turning into a criminal investigation," Joe said to his brother.

Snowdon stayed silent, his mouth tight. Frank could see something was bothering him. "What exactly was Henry Low River's grudge against Toby Gill?" he asked.

"Ten years ago, when Mr. Low River was living in Texas, he got a phone call from a man who called himself Todd Allan Miller. He said he wanted to build an art gallery in town to display all of Mr. Low River's wood sculptures. Miller sent him all kinds of official documents and blueprints. There were even real estate signs set out on the lot where the gallery was supposed to be built. My grand—" Snowdon suddenly stopped speaking.

"Mr. Low River was tricked into sending the man his life savings to help pay for the construction," Snowdon continued. "Once Miller cashed Mr. Low River's check, no one ever heard from him again. The real estate signs were phony, and the official documents turned out to be forged and worthless."

28

"But what does that have to do with Toby Gill?" Joe asked.

"When Mr. Low River first met Gill in Lone Wolf, he was convinced *he* was Todd Allan Miller," Snowdon replied. "He's threatened Gill in public, saying he was going to get justice one way or another."

"Why doesn't anyone believe Low River?" Frank wondered.

"Mr. Low River never saw this Miller guy in person," Snowdon explained. "Everything was done by mail or over the telephone. But he says he recognizes Gill's voice."

"Maybe we should check up on Toby Gill's background," Frank said, pushing in the clutch and waggling the stick shift, trying to find third gear on the rickety old truck.

"Sheriff San Dimas checked," Snowdon responded. "Toby Gill's been an insurance broker for twenty years. His reputation is spotless. And he was living in Missouri until a few years ago, so he can't be Todd Allan Miller."

"Low River had a motive for trashing Gill's office today—revenge—even if it was misguided," Joe pointed out. "And he is the only one we saw at the scene."

"It wasn't Henry Low River!" Snowdon snapped, raising his voice.

"How can you be so sure?" Joe asked.

"Because Henry Low River is my grandfather?" Snowdon said.

# 4 The Mystery Twister Strikes

Joe stared, dumbstruck, at the blond-haired, blue-eyed farmer. "I never would have guessed you were Native American."

"Only one-quarter," Snowdon replied. "When I was growing up, my parents seldom talked about our Cherokee heritage. I guess I still feel a little funny about it."

"Why?" Joe asked.

"There's still a lot of prejudice, even today," Snowdon explained. "Grandpa Henry and I hardly ever see each other. He lives in the Cherokee Nation, and, well . . ." Snowdon trailed off, looking out the window.

"Anything wrong?" Frank asked.

"If something bad *has* happened to Toby Gill," Snowdon replied, "everyone in town's going to think my grandfather is responsible. I'm pretty near dead sure he isn't responsible. I just hope I can prove it."

"We'd be glad to help," Joe offered. "We can follow a trail of clues as well as Bullet can follow a scent."

"And our hearing is a whole lot better," Frank joked, but Snowdon didn't laugh. "Even if your grandfather didn't harm Gill," Frank continued, "maybe he knows something about what happened to him."

Snowdon was silent for a moment. "Here's the car repair shop," he said to Frank, who pulled in front of the garage and parked.

"We need to hook up with Phil in Tulip," Joe said, "but maybe we can meet later and help you find your grandfather."

Snowdon looked away from the Hardys. "Between the farm and my truck, I have too many other things to worry about. Thanks for the ride." Snowdon got out of the truck and walked into the garage of the repair shop.

"Snowdon's been a little jumpy ever since we walked into Gill's insurance office," Frank noted.

"Especially after he saw his grandfather's station wagon pull away," Joe said. "There's more to this than we know."

"Maybe we can stop by and talk with Snowdon later, see if he'll open up," Frank said, putting the Blue Bomber in gear.

The rain had stopped, but Joe noticed that the

closer they got to Tulip, the darker and more gigantic the storm clouds grew. They were still three miles away from Tulip when Joe spotted the Windstormers' red bus and a dozen other vehicles, including a van from a local TV station. A growing crowd of onlookers surrounded the remains of a two-story wood-frame home.

"Turn here," Joe told his brother, spotting the long, unpaved red clay road that led to the ranch house.

"Check that out," Frank said, pointing to two cars beside the road. One had been flipped over on its side. The other had its front grille smashed in.

"There's Phil," Joe said as their pickup drew closer to the destroyed home.

Frank stopped near Phil, who was standing behind Mr. Jansen. The bearded scientist was kneeling beside a fallen tree, making notes. "Hi, Phil. Hey, Mr. Jansen!" Frank called out the window. "Are the people who were in those wrecked cars okay?"

"They're okay. Just some bumps and bruises," Jansen replied, not looking up from his work. "But it wasn't the tornado that did that. Those were two joyriders who tried to follow us here." Frank heard both anger and concern in Jansen's voice. The scientist shook his head. "I can't figure it out."

"I guess some people are just careless," Frank replied.

"No, I mean the debris pattern," Jansen said. "I can't figure it out."

Frank surveyed the area. Roof shingles, splintered furniture, broken glass, and hunks of plaster were strewn around all sides of the home. Only one of four walls remained standing. Water dripped from some twisted pipes, which Frank guessed had been attached to a bathtub on the second floor. On the land surrounding the house, half a dozen trees were uprooted.

With his newfound knowledge of twisters, Frank was able to make out the path the tornado had taken. "The debris pattern isn't to the left of the tornado's path," Frank noted.

"Correct," Jansen replied. "It's harum-scarum. Thrown about in every direction. I haven't seen anything like this since five years ago in New Mexico."

"The mystery twister?" Joe asked.

"The mystery twister," Jansen said, nodding.

"And Frank and I missed it," Joe said, frowning slightly to his brother.

"Apparently, we *all* missed it," Jansen told them. "No one besides the owner was in the area, and he was locked down in his storm shelter."

An attractive blond woman in a stylish blue business suit rushed over, followed by a cameraman toting a remote unit on his shoulder. "Mr. Jansen!" the woman shouted.

"Reporters," Jansen muttered. "Somehow they got here before we did."

"I'm Terry Clark, Channel Nine News," the newswoman said quickly, thrusting a microphone in Jansen's face. "Could you explain what happened here this afternoon?"

Jansen sighed wearily. "I'll tell you what I can, but then I have to get back to work."

Terry positioned Jansen so that the remains of the house were in the background, then began the interview. The boys stepped away from the camera to speak privately.

"Tornadoes in the Northern Hemisphere always move counterclockwise," Phil told his friends. "Mr. Jansen's theory is that some force of nature makes this particular kind of whirlwind change the direction of its rotation. But without an eyewitness, it's just guesswork."

"Sounds like the mystery twister is going to stay a mystery," Joe said.

"Even stranger," Phil said quietly. "Something jammed our Doppler radar so that we never got a read on this tornado. There's no data we can use to study it."

Joe saw a very tall, broad, balding man in a white linen suit step out of the rubble of the destroyed home. "Is that the owner?" he asked Phil.

Phil shook his head. "No. That's Alvin Bixby. He's an insurance salesman."

"I'm the owner," someone behind Joe said. Joe turned as a lean, lanky man in his forties with a lined, suntanned face and a worn Stetson hat stepped up and offered his hand to shake. "Hal Kanner's the name. I don't recognize you boys. Are you reporters or something?"

"No, they're friends of mine visiting from New York," Phil explained. "I'm an intern with Mr. Jansen's team."

"I see," Kanner replied.

Joe noticed Kanner was holding a ceramic piece of some kind. "What's that?"

"That's all that's left of a priceless Ming vase I had in my house," Kanner said grimly, holding up the broken porcelain piece.

"I'm sorry," Joe said, noticing the intricate design on the shard of pottery.

"Mr. Kanner!" Alvin Bixby called, waving for Kanner to join the crowd of onlookers that surrounded him.

"Okay, Mr. Bixby!" Kanner called back. "Excuse me, boys," Kanner said, tipping his hat and walking past them toward the crowd.

"Come on, Frank, let's see what's going on," Joe suggested. But he saw that Frank was inspecting the same fallen tree that Jansen had been looking at earlier.

"One second, Joe," Frank said. "Look at how the bark on the trunk has been scraped off. I wonder what caused that."

"Tornadoes can send bits of debris crashing into other objects at hundreds of miles an hour," Phil said. "Remember the nails in Snowdon's tires?"

Frank nodded, willing to accept Phil's explanation since he didn't have one of his own.

The boys joined the crowd of onlookers.

"Didn't you ever think to put your priceless valuables in a safe or something?" Bixby grumbled.

"What's the sense of owning beautiful pieces of art if you hide them away?" Kanner replied. Frank found it odd, hearing a hard-faced cowboy in denim jeans and a Stetson talking about beautiful pieces of art.

"It's careless!" Bixby scolded. "Leaving a priceless Ming vase on your fireplace mantel is just irresponsible. That's how my company is going to see it."

"Look here!" Kanner was steamed. "I insured my property, and by golly, you're going to make good on it!"

The crowd murmured their support of Kanner. Terry Clark moved in closer with her microphone.

"I never said we weren't going to pay up," Bixby said, trying to calm his client. "I'll send someone to assess the damage in the morning. We'll probably have a check for you by tomorrow afternoon."

"For how much?" Kanner asked.

"Your home and its contents appear to be a total loss. Based on the declared value of everything, I'd say the check will be for more than a million dollars."

A man in the crowd whistled. "A million and then some . . . My cousin lost his house in Lone Wolf this morning, and his insurance fellow won't even return his calls."

"United Insurers is one of the largest insurance companies in the country," Bixby explained. "They have large enough assets that they can compensate their customers almost immediately."

"With the prices you charge for insurance at United, you ought to pay out quick," another onlooker grumbled.

"I'm afraid that reflects the cost of doing business in an area as dangerous as Twister Alley," Bixby replied without emotion.

"I'm willing to pay extra to know my property is secured against tornado damage," a third person said. "Do you have a business card?"

"I don't know. I guess I have a few," Bixby replied, pulling a stack of business cards from his jacket pocket.

"A few business cards?" Joe noted. "He has enough to supply an army."

The crowd eagerly snatched up the cards, and Joe pushed to the front to be sure he got one before Bixby ran out.

"Hmm," Phil said, raising one eyebrow as he read the business card over Joe's shoulder. "His office is all the way on the other side of Lone Wolf."

An onlooker overheard Phil and called out to Bixby. "How'd you get here so fast?"

"I got in my car the minute Mr. Kanner phoned me with the bad news," Bixby replied. "That's how we're trained at United Insurers. Now, if you'll excuse me, there's some claim sites in Lone Wolf I need to visit."

Frank and Joe watched Bixby get into the driver's seat of his shiny white luxury car and drive off, passing the giant black truck belonging to Greg Glover, who was just now arriving on the scene.

"About time, Greg," Jansen said with a little smile as Glover jumped down five feet from the cab of his truck.

"You jammed our radar!" Glover accused, his face red with anger.

"We did not. Our radar transmissions were jammed, too, as a matter of fact," Jansen countered.

"Then how'd you find out about it?" Glover demanded.

"I got a phone call," Jansen replied.

"From who?" Glover asked.

"He didn't identify himself," Jansen said, shrugging.

"Baloney!" Glover shouted. "This is the lowest you've ever sunk, Jansen."

"I don't want to waste my time arguing with you!" Jansen bellowed. "An entirely unknown weather phenomenon touched down in our own backyard, and we both missed it!"

Frank watched Glover as the rival scientist pushed his black curly hair out of his eyes, quickly scanned the area, and within seconds concluded, "It's hit again."

"The mystery twister, as Frank calls it," Jansen said, nodding toward the older Hardy.

"Frank who? Do I know you?" Glover asked gruffly.

"Let's just say we nearly ran into each other this morning," Frank replied coolly.

"This thing doesn't seem to follow any of the rules," Jansen said. "It's cyclonic in nature, obviously—"

"I can see that," Glover interrupted. "Just like in New Mexico."

"How do you know about New Mexico?" Phil asked Glover.

"Greg and I used to work *together* in the good old days," Jansen said to Phil.

"Speak for yourself, Jansen," Glover snorted. "They weren't good old days for me. Whereas now I could buy and sell your whole outfit three times over."

"You've got the corporate backing, Greg," Jansen said, smiling, "but I have the magic. I'll solve this thing long before you do."

"We'll see about that," Glover said in a threatening tone. He stalked off to instruct the rest of his team, which was just now arriving.

"Nice guy," Joe said, shaking his head.

"The National Severe Storm Laboratories might have tracked it. I'll give them a call on my cell phone," Jansen said to Phil, closing his notebook and heading for the red bus.

"What's the National Severe Storm Laboratories?" Frank asked.

"The big boys," Phil replied. "The most advanced severe weather tracking facility in the country."

"What do you say to Frank and me helping your team analyze the debris?" Joe suggested to Phil, who was happy to show them the ropes.

While Joe and Phil began looking through the broken furnishings, Frank checked out a fallen telephone pole. It did not have the same markings as the fallen tree. Instead, there were two deep gouges in it, about five feet up from the ground. Inside the gouges, Frank could see red clay residue.

Joe picked up a broken piece of pottery. It looked like fine porcelain and had exactly the same colors and pattern on it as Kanner's Ming vase. When Joe turned it over, he saw some tiny lettering on it. "Occupied Japan," he said aloud. "I wonder what that means."

"What did you find?" a voice behind them asked. Joe and Phil turned to find Kanner moving in closer, craning his neck to get a look at the porcelain fragment.

"It's another piece of your Ming vase, I think," Phil answered.

"Let me see that," Kanner said, holding out his hand, palm up, for Joe to give it to him.

Out of the corner of his eye, Joe noticed what he thought was a large white bug jumping in the grass. Then another, and another. Joe realized they were not bugs but small hailstones, which were beginning to rain down from the dark thunderhead above them.

Joe began to hand Kanner the porcelain piece, then hesitated. "Do you mind if I keep it as a souvenir of the tornado?"

"Yes, I do mind," Kanner said sharply, extending his hand farther. "Hand it over."

Suddenly, the sky erupted in a full-scale hailstorm. Joe and the others were bombarded with chunks of ice the size of golf balls. There were shouts coming from every direction as people headed for shelter.

"Run for cover!" Frank yelled as he bolted for the blue pickup truck.

"No!" Phil shouted after him. "There might be another tornado on the way. Let's head for the storm shelter!"

Joe turned away from Kanner, joining Phil and Frank as they ran to the shelter. Frank pulled on the shelter door. It budged one inch, then stopped. Frank saw it was chained and padlocked shut.

"No good," Frank told the other two.

"Over there!" Joe shouted, pointing to a small concrete pump house near the barbed-wire fence that marked the boundary of Kanner's property. The hailstones were now as big as lemons and struck the boys' backs and shoulders with the force of hard punches.

Frank arrived first at the pump house. After flinging open the door, he squeezed into the tight space beside the iron pipes of the pumping mechanism that supplied water to the farm. Phil squeezed in behind Frank.

Joe was trailing. He was only ten yards from the pump house when he was shoved from behind and into the barbed-wire fence. The piece of porcelain went flying out of his hand.

As Joe rose from the ground, he was tripped by a string of barbed wire wrapped around his right foot. The wind whipped with gale force.

Just as he was reaching down to untangle himself, Joe was struck on the back of the head by a baseball-size hailstone. The force knocked him to the ground. He lay there, unable to move, nearly unconscious—and knowing that a tornado was going to touch down at any second.

# 5 Blown Away

"Where's Joe?" Frank shouted. "I have to go get him!"

The rain and hail were so heavy, Frank couldn't see two feet beyond the pump house door. Pushing past Phil, Frank reemerged from his safe shelter to look for his brother.

Immediately, Frank was struck in the back by giant hailstones and driven to his knees. Though the wind was knocked out of him, he pushed forward, crawling toward the figure he could barely make out lying on the ground near the fence.

Frank found Joe nearly unconscious. Pulling the barbed wire away from Joe's foot, Frank reached beneath his brother's arms and clasped his hands across Joe's chest. Frank then backpedaled against the wind toward the shelter, dragging Joe with him.

Phil helped Frank get Joe into the pump house and closed the door. "Is he all right?" Phil asked.

Frank checked Joe, feeling the lump on the back of his head. "Looks like something hit him."

"Hail," Joe muttered.

"What?" Phil said, leaning closer.

"Hail. I was hit by a piece the size of Mount Rushmore," Joe joked, having regained his senses. "I'm okay, I think."

Frank touched the sore spots on his back. "I suddenly have more respect for the Blue Bomber. I've only been through one hailstorm, and I'm ready for the body shop."

"Somebody pushed me into the barbed wire," Joe said, sitting up.

"Pushed you?" Frank asked.

"I'm sure of it," Joe said, wincing as he touched the bump.

The wind howled outside. "What's our best move, Phil?" Frank asked.

"To stay here until it passes over," Phil replied, knocking on the concrete wall. "This is probably the safest place on the whole farm."

The wind soon died down. As the boys emerged from their cover, they saw that little more damage had occurred.

Jansen walked over, soaking wet and holding

the lid to an ice cooler over his head. Frank figured he had used it as a shield against hailstones. "Nothing touched down," Jansen grumbled to the boys. "I guess it just isn't my lucky day."

Frank and Joe shared a smile over the eccentric scientist's reckless obsession with tornadoes.

Thirty minutes later the skies had cleared. "Hard to believe how quickly the weather can change," Frank said to his brother as he buttoned up the dry denim shirt he had retrieved from his suitcase.

"No kidding," Joe replied, toweling off his wet hair. He suddenly remembered something. "The piece of vase. I dropped it when I fell."

"Let's take a look," Frank suggested.

Phil and the Hardys scoured every inch of ground surrounding the pump house and the section of fence where Joe had fallen, but they could find no trace of the broken piece.

"The storm must have blown it away," Phil concluded. "You're sure it said 'Occupied Japan'?"

"Positive," Joe replied.

Jansen joined them by the pump house. "We're finished here, Phil. Let's get back to headquarters."

"Mr. Jansen?" Frank asked. "What do you know about Ming vases?"

"They were made in China during the Ming dynasty," Jansen replied. "That's about all I know."

"Have you heard of Occupied Japan?" Joe asked.

"Yes," Jansen replied. "But what does that have to do with Ming vases?"

"Oh," Joe said thoughtfully. "I thought it might be possible that a Ming vase could have been made in Occupied Japan."

Jansen laughed. "Most definitely not, Joe. The Ming dynasty was thousands of years ago. Occupied Japan existed for only a short period after World War Two."

Joe exchanged a look with Frank. "I think there's more than unusual debris patterns that need to be explained here."

The boys told Jansen about the piece of porcelain they had discovered.

"Let me take a look at it," Jansen said.

"Problem," Joe replied. "We lost it. But we're trying to find it now."

Just then everyone's attention was taken by Kanner, whose shouting could be heard from thirty yards away. "I'm too upset to have everybody wandering all over my property, gawking at my misfortune. Now git!"

The neighbors, newspeople, and storm chasers all began to gather their things and reluctantly cleared the property. Phil started up the Blue Bomber, and he and the Hardys followed Jansen's red bus back toward Lone Wolf and Wind-stormer headquarters.

Joe noticed a white tractor-trailer parked along the shoulder on a side road. It was the same truck that had sped by them on their way in from the airport. The driver, a man with long black hair and a mustache, was casually leaning against the rear bumper.

"He sure was in a hurry to get nowhere," Joe commented.

"Yeah," Frank said, rubbing his bottom lip. "I wonder what that's all about."

The Windstormers were headquartered in a modest group of buildings that, Phil explained, used to be part of an old ranch. He showed the Hardys to their "room," a corner of an equipment storage area where two sleeping bags had been rolled out. "This used to be a dog kennel. The old owners bred sheepdogs."

"That's comforting to know," Joe said.

"Sorry, guys. Not much extra space at Club Jansen," their friend said, laughing.

"Honestly, Phil, it's fine," Frank said. "We'll be happy to sit quietly for a few hours."

"Cool," Phil said. "Because it's my turn to clean the bathrooms."

Joe laughed. "Hey, who said being an intern wasn't glamorous?"

Phil showed the boys to the kitchen before leaving them. After grabbing two sandwiches and a couple of sodas from the refrigerator, Frank and Joe sat down to sort through all the strange happenings in Lone Wolf and Tulip that day.

"In Tulip," Frank began, "we have Hal Kanner trying to collect on a fishy insurance claim."

"And in Lone Wolf," Joe continued, "we have the disappearance of Toby Gill."

Frank posed a question to his brother. "Who would benefit from Toby Gill being out of the way?"

"Henry Low River," Joe replied through a mouthful of ham and cheese. "It would satisfy his grudge."

"Or Alvin Bixby," Frank suggested, "the other insurance guy. That's certainly one way of getting rid of the competition."

"Let's work on the Kanner problem first," Joe suggested, sucking down the rest of his soda. "I'd like to inspect the Kanner farm more closely, when there aren't so many people around."

"Good idea. The whole tornado aftermath seemed scripted," Frank said.

"Scripted?" Joe asked.

"Yeah. Too perfect," Frank explained. "Not a single witness to verify Kanner's story. If we can find some more hard evidence that Kanner is trying to collect money on works of art that were never destroyed, we can bring it to Sheriff San Dimas."

Joe nodded and finished off his sandwich.

Things were quiet in the Windstormer control

room as Joe and Frank stopped behind a radar screen manned by Diana Lucas.

"What's the forecast?" Frank asked.

"It stinks," Diana replied. "There's a break in the weather. Zero percent chance of tornadoes until at least tomorrow afternoon."

"Bummer," Joe said. "Did Mr. Jansen find out anything from the National Severe Storm Laboratories?"

"Something jammed their radar reception, too," Diana replied. "The trouble only lasted for five minutes. NSSL pinpointed the location—about three miles from the Kanner farm—but when they sent the authorities there to investigate, all they found was an empty field."

"That means no one has any images of the mystery twister," Joe said.

"Why would someone jam radar transmissions?" Frank wondered.

"For the same reason some hackers break into a corporation's computers and plant viruses," Diana replied. "To prove that they can."

"And to prove that they're jerks," Joe added.

Phil walked in, wearing rubber gloves and carrying a mop and a bucket. "Finished!"

"Take a breather, Phil," Diana said. "Nothing to do around here till tomorrow."

"Phil, you're a technology buff," Frank began. "How would someone jam radar transmissions?"

"Simple," Phil responded. "You can rig a microwave oven—"

"That wouldn't affect an area this vast," Diana said. "You would need the kind of jammer they use in the military."

"Hmm. Why don't we take a drive, Phil?" Frank proposed.

"Are there some sights you'd like to see?" Phil asked.

"One," Frank replied. "The site of the mystery twister."

By the time Phil and the Hardys reached the red clay road leading to the Kanner farm, the sun was beginning to set. The place seemed completely deserted now. Phil parked the Blue Bomber behind a grouping of trees so that it couldn't be seen from the highway.

"I'm glad we thought to bring these," Joe said, grabbing a flashlight and handing two more to Frank and Phil. "This is real country darkness out here."

"Why are we here, exactly?" Phil asked as they walked down the clay drive.

"Remember how nervous Kanner got when I found that phony piece of Ming vase?" Joe said.

"You don't think that he just misidentified it?" Phil asked.

"Let's put it this way. Frank and I think there may have been more than Mother Nature at work out here today," Joe said. "And if we snoop around here, maybe we can find some proof."

Frank's flashlight beam fell on the padlocked

door to the storm shelter. "I noticed this earlier, and it still doesn't make sense," he said.

"What doesn't?" Joe asked.

"Why would Hal Kanner go to the trouble of padlocking his storm shelter right after a tornado has leveled his house?" Frank said.

"I would be thinking about the valuable stuff I wanted to salvage," Phil said.

"Exactly," Frank said.

"Do you think he's hiding something down there?" Joe asked.

Frank shook his head. "Take a look. The keyhole on the lock is rusted over. I doubt it's been opened in years."

"Then Kanner was lying about being in the storm shelter when the twister hit," Joe said.

Frank nodded and pulled his penknife from his pocket. "It's an old lock. I might be able to pick it." Frank scraped away the rust and wiggled the point of the blade back and forth in the keyhole. Finally, the lock popped open.

Cobwebs stretched across the staircase leading down into the small shelter. "As I thought, no one's been in this shelter in a long time," Frank remarked. "You and Phil check inside what's left of the house, and I'll check the grounds."

On every fallen tree, Frank found the same marks where something had scraped off the bark. Beneath one tree, Frank noticed a patch of red clay that had been sheltered from the rain. In it

51

he could make out the track of a tractor tire. That's odd, Frank thought. Kanner doesn't appear to own a tractor or have a barn where he could keep one.

Frank was surprised by how dark it had gotten so quickly. He stumbled in a depression in the ground. Shining his flashlight downward, he saw that his foot had caught in some deep tire tracks. They were double tracks, like the type made by a tractor-trailer, and so deep, Frank guessed, it must have been a truck loaded down with cargo.

As he moved on toward the black silhouette of another fallen tree, he realized it was, in fact, a telephone pole. He traced the length of the pole with his flashlight beam. The telephone wires had been torn in half when it fell. So how did Kanner call Bixby to tell him about the twister? Frank wondered.

Meanwhile, Joe moved carefully through the shambles of the Kanner house, balancing on broken planks and fallen beams. An elaborate gilded picture frame caught his eye, and he pulled it from beneath a pile of broken glass and rubble.

The broken frame looked ancient, and the portrait was of a man dressed as a Pilgrim. Shining his flashlight on the edge of the torn canvas, Joe noticed something odd. Although the back of the canvas was brown and faded, the torn edge revealed a bright white canvas beneath it.

"Take a look at this, Phil," Joe called to his friend.

Phil examined the canvas closely. "The canvas looks new. It looks like it was just stained to make it look old."

"In other words, it looks like a forgery, right?" Joe asked.

Phil nodded. "Maybe Kanner really is up to something."

They heard a creaking noise from another room. Phil and Joe stood frozen for a moment, listening. There was a faint sound, like steam rushing through a pipe.

"Sounds like the house is still shifting," Phil whispered.

Joe sniffed the air. A strange smell was filling the area.

"Yuck," Phil said, putting his hand over his nose. "What is it?"

"Propane," Joe replied.

Frank was moving toward the house, eager to tell the others what he had discovered, when he noticed a small fire erupt over near the pump house. The flames spread quickly, following a thin trail of flammable material leading straight to the ruins of the house.

"Joe, Phil! Run for it!" Frank screamed at the top of his lungs. "The house is going to blow!"

# 6 Up in Flames

Hearing Frank's warning, Joe turned and, through a broken window, spotted the trail of flames speeding toward the house.

"This way!" he shouted to Phil. But as they tried to hopscotch through the piled-up debris, a fallen section of wall gave way under Phil. His leg crashed through the hole and stuck fast.

Joe saw that the flame trail had reached the edge of the house. Broken glass and splintered wood surrounded Phil, but Joe knew there was no time to be delicate. He roughly yanked Phil's leg back through the hole with his muscular arms and carried his friend beyond the piled-up clutter.

"Over here!" Frank yelled, motioning to Joe as he and Phil emerged from the building. Frank opened the shelter door and moved to help his friend and his brother.

"I can walk!" Phil shouted. Joe let him down, and the two boys ran full-steam for the shelter. Joe and Phil leaped through the spiderwebs covering the doorway, tumbling down the stairs.

As Frank tried to follow, he heard a massive explosion and felt burning heat on his back. The force of the explosion threw him down the stairs and on top of Joe, who cushioned his fall.

The ground outside caught fire, fueled by the bits of debris. The wooden door of the shelter was on fire.

"I'll shut the door!" Phil shouted, heading up the stairs.

"No! If we stay down here, we'll be baked like clams," Frank realized.

Joe nodded. "Let's make a break for it."

The three boys rushed up the stairs and zig-zagged through narrow paths of wet ground that had not caught on fire. Reaching safety, they turned back to look at the blaze.

"There goes the Kanner farmhouse," Frank said.

Joe leaned over, hands on his knees, trying to catch his breath. "And with it, all our evidence."

Phil used the CB in the Blue Bomber to radio for help. Fifteen minutes later it was not a fire engine but a water tanker truck and eight civilians in cars that showed up on the scene.

"Tulip Volunteer Fire Department!" a gray-haired man in a yellow raincoat announced.

Sheriff San Dimas and a deputy pulled up in their squad car. "Holy cow, how'd this get started?" San Dimas asked.

"No time now, Sheriff," the gray-haired man said. "We're going to need every man if we're going to get this fire under control."

San Dimas nodded and grabbed two buckets from one of the volunteers' trunks.

"We'll be glad to help you put it out, too," Joe offered.

"We don't have enough water to put it out, son," the gray-haired man told Joe, handing him a shovel. "We need to control it and let it burn out on its own."

While Joe, Frank, and Phil helped the volunteers dig a ditch, or firebreak, encircling one-half of the fire, the tanker truck pumped water to soak the ground in front of the other side of the flame wall. Unable to spread any farther, the fire burned itself out in a couple of hours.

The gray-haired firefighter came walking out of the charred remains of the house and reported to San Dimas. "Looks like the tornado ruptured the gas main. Then something touched it off."

Sheriff San Dimas looked at Frank. "Any idea what that something was?"

"It was arson," Frank told San Dimas, and led him to the spot near the scorched pump house where he had seen the fire erupt.

56

San Dimas looked at the burned, blackened ground that surrounded them. "If there was any evidence it was started on purpose, it'll be hard to find now."

The boys told San Dimas their suspicions about Hal Kanner—about the call that he claimed he made even though his phone lines were down, the unused storm shelter he said he was hiding in when the twister hit, the unexplained tire tracks, the apparent forged painting, and the Ming vase fragment inscribed "Occupied Japan."

"It does sound fishy," San Dimas agreed. "Do you have the painting or the vase fragment?"

Joe and Frank frowned and shook their heads. "They're in there," Joe said, nodding in the direction of the house.

"Maybe we can still dig something out of this mess," San Dimas said. "I'll station Deputy Klement here for the night and come back at first daylight to take a closer look. Right now, I have some other problems to deal with. Toby Gill is still missing, and there's been no answer at Henry Low River's place all day. I'm headed out to Tahlequah right now to try to find him."

"Shouldn't somebody tell Mr. Kanner about the fire?" Klement asked.

"Just in case he forgot that he started it," Joe said under his breath to Phil.

"Mr. Kanner didn't start it," the deputy said sharply. "I saw him through the window of the diner when we were leaving Lone Wolf."

"He's probably staying at the Sandman Motel tonight," San Dimas said.

"How do you know?" Joe wondered.

"Because it's the only motel in a twenty-mile radius," San Dimas replied.

"We're headed back to town," Frank offered. "We can give Mr. Kanner the message."

San Dimas considered Frank and his friends for a moment. "That better be all you do. Just give him the message."

The boys nodded. In the Blue Bomber, they followed San Dimas down the clay road and onto the two-lane highway.

"Are you really just going to give Kanner the message about the fire?" Phil asked.

"Sure," Frank replied with a smile. "I just might ask him a few questions first."

They followed the squad car until San Dimas turned onto the road that led to Tahlequah. A few seconds later, Joe recognized Snowdon's pickup as it passed by them. Turning his head, Joe saw the pickup turn onto the same road as San Dimas.

"That was Snowdon," Joe informed his friends. "Looks like he's headed out to the Cherokee Nation, too. So much for not having time to look for his grandfather."

"I know you like to be where the action is, Joe," Frank said.

"Yeah, I do, but what about Hal Kanner?" Joe wondered.

"Drop me off in town," Frank suggested. "I'll find out what I can about Hal Kanner, while you and Phil see what Snowdon's up to."

Phil and Joe let Frank off in front of the Prairie Moon Diner in Lone Wolf, then made a U-turn and headed back up the road toward Tahlequah.

The bell on the door jingled as Frank walked into the tiny establishment. The place was almost empty. He didn't see Kanner but was surprised to see someone else. "Diana?"

Diana Lucas, in a pink waitress uniform, smiled when she saw Frank. "Hey, one of the Hardys! Have a seat."

"I didn't know you—" Frank began.

"Yeah," Diana broke in. "My uncle owns the place. I moonlight here for extra bucks when he needs me."

Frank sat in the first booth. "I was looking for Hal Kanner. Do you know him?"

Diana ignored the question and flipped open her order pad. "What can I get you?"

"How about an order of fries and a little information?" Frank replied.

"No problem on the fries," Diana said, turning away and handing the order to the cook.

"Deputy Klement said he saw Kanner in here," Frank mentioned.

"Yeah?" Diana answered.

"Is there anything you could tell me about him?" Frank went on. "About his art collection or who his friends are?"

"It's none of my business," she replied.

"How about less personal information?" Frank said, smiling warmly. "Do you know if he owns a cellular phone or a Mack truck?"

"Listen, Frank, or Joe, or whichever one you are," Diana said coolly. "I don't talk to strangers, especially when they act real friendly and smile too much."

With that, Diana walked away and disappeared into the back room. Frank looked after her. He wasn't quite sure what he had done to upset her.

"Don't take it personally," the cook said. "Her family lost their farm in Iowa because some smooth talker suckered her dad into buying bogus flood insurance. She doesn't trust people much anymore."

"Thanks," Frank said.

"I'm Oscar Lucas, Diana's uncle," the cook said, coming out from behind the counter and shaking Frank's hand. "I own the diner."

"I'm Frank Hardy," Frank replied.

"Why do you want to know about Kanner?" Lucas asked.

Frank gave Lucas a brief rundown of the happenings at the Kanner farm. "So there are a lot of questions that need answering."

"Well, the deputy was right," Lucas explained. "Kanner was in here tonight, talking to the head of the local bank."

"What about?" Frank asked.

"Selling his property," Lucas replied. "Kanner

was so upset about losing his house, he planned to pack up and leave Twister Alley altogether."

"And the bank's going to buy the property?" Frank asked.

"Kanner was willing to sell it cheap," Lucas told him as he pulled the basket out of the deep fryer and dumped Frank's fries onto a plate. "If I overheard correctly, he's coming into the bank tomorrow morning to sign over the deed and get his money."

"Sounds like he's in a hurry to collect and leave," Frank muttered, half to himself. "Did you see where Mr. Kanner went when he left?"

"Right across the street to the Sandman Motel," Lucas told him. "You want anything else, Frank?" Lucas asked as he walked toward the front door with his keys. "I'm closing up."

Frank shook his head and looked up as Diana returned from the back room. "I'm sorry, Frank," she said in a gentler tone. "I don't know why I got so upset."

"Probably because I got too nosy," Frank replied. They both smiled.

"I've locked up the front," Lucas said. "Hope you don't mind leaving by the back way."

"Not at all," Frank said as he followed Diana and her uncle into the back room. Diana was turning off the lights, when Frank noticed a window looking out onto the alley behind Toby Gill's office.

"Can I be nosy just a little bit more?" Frank

61

asked. "Toby Gill wasn't in his office this morning—"

"Yeah, I saw him leave," Lucas offered. Frank was struck speechless by the sudden answer. "About nine-thirty Toby loaded three boxes of stuff into the trunk of his car and took off."

"Wow!" Frank exclaimed. "Then Henry Low River had nothing to do with his disappearance."

"I wouldn't go so far as to say that," Lucas said, frowning. "Henry was parked down the alley and started to follow him."

"You're certain it was Mr. Low River?" Frank asked.

"I had a clear view of his face," Lucas replied. "He rolled down his window to toss something out."

"What did he toss out, Uncle Oscar?" Diana asked, getting pulled into the story.

"Some little green box," Lucas replied. "It should still be there."

"Would you mind showing me where he threw it?" Frank asked.

Lucas took Frank to the spot. Sure enough, there was a small green box in the gutter.

"Uh-oh," Frank said as he picked it up.

"Why 'uh-oh'?" Diana asked. "What is it, Frank?"

Frank looked up at her and her uncle. "It's an empty box of thirty-eight-caliber cartridges."

# 7 A Hidden Fugitive

Joe and Phil were already in Tahlequah before they realized that they had a problem: They didn't know where they were going. Joe spotted a brightly lit building coming up on the right.

"Stop at this convenience store," Joe instructed. Phil pulled over, and Joe got out and walked into the store. He immediately felt that all eyes were on him. The clerk and all the customers were Native American.

"Hi! How ya doing?" Joe said cheerfully. "Do any of you know where a wood sculptor named Henry Low River lives?"

After a pause, the clerk replied. "No. Sorry." The others just continued staring at Joe. He had never felt more like an outsider.

"Thank you anyway," Joe said with a smile,

then turned and left. He passed a young Native American boy outside who was sitting on his bicycle and munching on a candy bar. Joe was about to get back into the pickup when he changed his mind and walked back.

"Excuse me—could I ask you something?" he asked the boy.

"Sure. What's up?" the boy replied without hesitation.

"I'm looking for a Mr. Low River. He's a sculptor," Joe told him.

"I know him," the boy said. "Go down five blocks to Red Rock and take a left."

"What's the address?" Joe asked.

"I don't know, but you can't miss it," the boy replied, grinning.

When Phil came to a stop in front of Henry Low River's house on Red Rock Road, Joe understood why the young boy had been grinning. The front yard was filled with animals in every size, shape, and species imaginable, all carved in wood.

"There's the sheriff's car," Phil said, nodding to the squad car parked in the street.

"And that's the green station wagon we saw this morning," Joe added, pointing to an open garage.

Joe noticed the faint smell of hickory smoke in the air. As he and Phil walked past an eight-foot-high grizzly bear and a life-size moose, metal chimes hanging on the eaves of the house clanged softly in the breeze.

The place looked dark inside, but Joe knocked anyway. "No answer," he said after a moment.

"I guess we should leave, then." Phil rubbed his arms as if he were cold, even though it was warm out. Joe could tell his friend was nervous.

"I would hate to have to go in uninvited," Joe said, eyes scanning the area for a possible way inside.

"Me, too. It's called breaking and entering, Joe," Phil said.

Joe tried the front door. The knob turned. "It's unlocked," he whispered.

"Great. The sheriff might reduce the charge to trespassing, then," Phil said.

Joe knew Phil was right. "Good call, Phil. There's no reason for us to break the law."

"Why don't we ask the neighbors?" Phil suggested. "Maybe they know where Mr. Low River is."

Phil grabbed a flashlight from the truck, and they walked through Low River's side yard. Joe spotted Snowdon's pickup truck parked behind the neighboring house. "Check it out, Phil," Joe said quietly to his friend.

Phil clicked off his flashlight and pulled Joe down with him to a squatting position. They watched from the cover of the tall grass as a figure walked out of a wooded area behind the homes on Red Rock Road. As the man opened the door to the pickup, the interior light illuminated his face. It was Snowdon.

"Whew!" Phil said as he flipped on the flashlight again.

"Snowdon," Joe called.

Snowdon jerked his head around. "Joe? What are you doing here?"

Joe saw Snowdon quickly toss a crumpled bag on the front seat and close the door. "The sheriff hasn't been able to reach your grandfather on the phone all day," Joe said, stretching the truth just a bit. "We thought we might be able to help find him."

"Thanks, Joe. I'm concerned myself," Snowdon said, looking down at his feet. "I've asked all over for him. No one seems to know anything."

Joe thought Snowdon seemed nervous. "We were afraid you would be too overwhelmed with your other problems to get out here."

"Oh, yeah, well, a couple of my neighbors are organizing a barnraising for tomorrow," Snowdon said. "The whole community's going to pitch in to rebuild our barn in one day."

"It doesn't look like there'll be any tornadoes to chase," Phil said, "so you can count us in, too."

"Good," Snowdon replied. He shifted on his feet. "Well, it's late. We'd better all get home and get some sleep."

"Are you okay, Snowdon?" Joe asked.

"Sure!" Snowdon replied, perking up and clap-

ping Joe on the back. When he did, Joe got a
whiff of the young farmer's shirt. It had the
strong scent of hickory smoke on it.

"Phil, tell Snowdon about the mystery twister," Joe suggested. While Phil was talking, Joe
slipped around to the other side of the pickup,
reached through the passenger window, and
grabbed the crumpled bag off the seat. As he did,
Snowdon opened the door on the driver's side.

"What are you doing, Joe?" Snowdon asked.

"Just checking out your tires," Joe replied.
"They look good as new."

"They *are* new," Snowdon said, looking a bit
confused.

"Well, then, that's a good thing," Joe said.

Snowdon smiled. "We'll see you in the
morning."

After Snowdon pulled away, Phil began heading for the Blue Bomber. "Wait a second, Phil,"
Joe called after him. Joe looked in the crumpled
bag. There was a crumpled root beer can, an
apple core, an empty bag of chips, and a crust of
bread.

"Well, we know what his eating habits are,"
Joe said. He looked toward the grove of trees. "I
have a hunch, Phil. Snowdon's hiding something,
and I think I know what it is. Come on."

As Joe and Phil walked toward the grove of
trees, the smell of hickory became sharper. At
the center of the grove, they came upon on an old
wooden shack. "It's a smokehouse," Joe quietly

told his friend. "And it's my guess that Henry Low River is hiding inside it."

"Okay," Phil said. "And I suppose you want to go in and find him?"

Joe smiled and nodded yes. Phil shook his head no. When Joe didn't budge, Phil sighed, then nodded as well. Phil opened the door, and they slipped in. Hams hung from hooks, as did a lit lantern and some sides of bacon. Hickory chips smoldered in a long rectangular barbecue grill that ran along the back wall. But there was no sign of Henry Low River.

"I guess I was wrong," Joe said. "Let's go."

Just then, Joe felt something creak beneath him. He looked down to see the floorboards moving. Before he could run to safety or even move an inch, he found himself falling through the floor!

# 8 The Wrong Gun

Joe hit the bottom of the five-foot-deep pit with a thud. Phil knelt and stuck his head through the trapdoor. "Joe, what happened? You okay?"

A hand reached up from the shadows and yanked Phil by the collar down into the pit. Joe saw the gleam of the blade of an ivory-handled pocketknife that was being brandished at Phil. As his eyes became accustomed to the light, he also saw the long handle of a Colt .45 revolver in their attacker's other hand.

"Who are you?" the voice asked from the shadows.

"Joe Hardy," Joe replied.

"Phil Cohen," his friend said, a tremble in his voice. "Harmless, nonviolent Phil Cohen."

"Let me guess. You're Henry Low River?" Joe

69

asked. The man didn't answer. "You're holding the knife that your grandson picked up off the floor in Toby Gill's office, so I'm pretty sure I'm right."

"What if you are?" the man asked.

"We're not the law," Joe assured him. "We're just trying to help find out what happened to Toby Gill."

In one quick movement, the man pushed Phil over to Joe's side of the pit. He folded his pocket-knife against his chest and put it away. He kept the gun trained on the two boys.

As the man leaned into the light, Joe got a good look at him. Low River looked younger than Joe had expected, maybe fifty. He had a strong face, with imposing features and wrinkles around the eyes. His hair was long and black with silver strands.

"I'll tell you where Gill is," Low River said. "He's running. He cruised, the same way he did after he rooked me in Texas."

"If that's true, what were you doing parked behind his office this morning?" Joe asked.

"Hanging out. Hoping he might come back for something," Low River said. "I had gone to his office earlier to flush him out."

"Flush him out?" Phil asked.

"To make him fess up to being the crook that he is," Low River said. "I brought my Colt along in case he needed persuading."

"What did Gill do when you confronted him?" Joe asked.

"Never happened, man," Low River grumbled. "When I got there, he was packing up his car like his house was on fire. He saw me and burned rubber. I burned rubber after him. I trailed him as far as the Dust Bowl Truck Stop, then he disappeared."

"You mean you lost him when he walked into the truck stop?" Joe asked.

"No, man. I mean he drove around the back and went *poof*. Him, his car, everything," Low River told him. "So I headed back to his office, just in case Gill had spaced out and forgotten something."

"You have an interesting way of talking," Phil said.

Low River grinned. "Hey, I'm fifty percent Cherokee but one hundred percent old hippie."

Joe didn't feel quite as threatened by Henry Low River. "Mr. Low River, would you mind . . ." Joe nodded toward the revolver.

"Hm? Oh, yeah. This thing," Low River said, looking at the revolver. "Shows you what I know about firesticks. I ended up buying the wrong bullets."

"You mean . . . ?" Phil started to ask.

"Yeah, it's not even loaded," Low River said with a grin.

"But this *is* loaded," a voice above them said.

71

Sheriff San Dimas stood over them in the smoke-house, pointing his firearm at Low River. "Drop it, Henry."

Joe had mixed feelings about being rescued from his situation. He now found it hard to believe that Low River could have hurt Toby Gill.

"Mr. Low River has an explanation to cover everything," he said to San Dimas, who was leading Low River away from the smokehouse in handcuffs.

"Yeah, he usually does," San Dimas remarked. Joe and Phil followed as San Dimas took his captive to the edge of a nearby river that ran behind the woods and began to walk along the bank.

"Don't be fooled, Joe. This guy is trouble. Last December, he slashed all four of Toby Gill's tires."

"Hey, when the law won't punish a criminal," Low River said to San Dimas, "it's up to the common citizen to do what can be done."

"In February," San Dimas went on, "Henry blew up Toby's toolshed with a stick of dyna-mite."

"You never proved that," Low River insisted with a grin.

"The joke's over, Henry," San Dimas said solemnly. Up ahead Joe saw a tow truck backing up to the edge of a river. Sticking out of the water was the rear fender and taillight of a cream-colored automobile.

"Recognize that car?" San Dimas asked Low River.

Low River stared, shaking his head, until he finally found his voice. "It's Toby Gill's."

Low River told his story—how he had followed Gill to the truck stop and lost him. As bad as Joe thought it looked for Low River then, it looked worse after the tow truck pulled Gill's car onto the embankment. There was a bullet hole in the window of the driver's side and another hole in the seat.

"If Toby Gill was sitting in the driver's seat when that shot was fired," San Dimas said, "we may have more than a kidnapping on our hands."

"I don't know anything about this," Low River said vehemently.

"Your neighbor remembers seeing this car drive up to your house at about two this afternoon," San Dimas reported. "He didn't see who was driving, but twenty minutes later he heard a gunshot. When he looked out his window, the car wasn't there anymore."

"No way, man! I'm being framed!" Low River shouted.

Joe knew he should tell the sheriff about Mr. Low River's pocketknife, but he decided to keep the information to himself for now.

As the tow truck hoisted up the rear tires of

73

Gill's car, Joe noticed a large, heavy polished rock jammed against the gas pedal. "Look at this," he said. "This rock was probably used as a weight to press down the gas pedal when the perpetrator drove the car into the river, but what exactly is it?"

"A petrified wood paperweight," Phil told his friend. "They sell them in souvenir shops all around here."

Joe saw a gold pen holder attached to the paperweight. The pen itself appeared to be missing.

"Henry, you're going to have to come in with me for questioning," San Dimas said. He helped Low River into the back of his squad car, got into the front, and drove away.

Joe shined the flashlight on his watch. It was after midnight. "I think it's time to call it a day, Phil."

"Good idea, Joe," his friend agreed wearily.

Back at Windstormer headquarters, Joe and Phil hooked up with Frank, who filled them in on what he had found out about Kanner selling his property. "I also went by the Sandman Motel. Kanner rented a room there, but no one answered when I knocked."

"I'm guessing Kanner's going to take the money and run," Joe said. "If we could just keep him in town long enough to prove our suspicions about him."

74

"Let's talk to Alvin Bixby in the morning before he hands over that fat insurance check to Kanner," Frank suggested. "If Bixby will delay paying him even for a few days, it might be long enough for us to get to the bottom of this."

"We need to tell you about Toby Gill," Phil told Frank.

"Toby Gill!" Frank exclaimed, smacking his forehead. "Wait till you hear what *I* found out. Oscar Lucas saw Gill packing up and leaving his office this morning. Low River followed him and threw an empty box of thirty-eight cartridges out his window as he passed the diner."

"Thirty-eight caliber?" Joe said. "So maybe Mr. Low River was telling the truth about buying the wrong bullets." Joe saw the confused look on his brother's face and quickly told Frank about the events of the night.

"The evidence is mounting against Mr. Low River," Phil said, "and either Snowdon is involved, or he's trying to cover up for his grandfather."

"Unless Mr. Low River really is being framed," Joe countered, "and Snowdon is just trying to protect him."

"If we believe Low River, Joe, that means Toby Gill is a swindler and was probably closing shop and leaving town this morning," Frank said.

"But why?" Phil wondered.

"Remember when I asked who would profit

from Toby Gill's disappearance?" Frank said. "There was one person we forgot to mention: Toby Gill himself."

"Of course," Joe said. "He collects thousands of dollars in insurance premiums and then skips town before he has to pay out on any damages."

"Insurance doesn't work that way," Phil pointed out. "Gill is just a salesman working for a big insurance company. The customers' fees are paid to the parent company, and then when the customers have claims, the parent company pays them off, not Gill."

Joe frowned. Phil's information put a damper on his theory.

Frank recalled the story he had heard in the diner. "Diana Lucas's family lost their farm because they had bought phony flood insurance from a swindler. What if Gill was doing the same thing—selling false tornado insurance policies and somehow pocketing the money?"

"It would explain why he would disappear the moment the first tornado hit town," Joe said.

"But San Dimas ran a check on Gill," Phil reminded them. "He's been an honest salesman for twenty years. Why would he suddenly turn criminal?"

Frank paused for a moment. "I admit I'm stumped. We need to find out more about Gill and his insurance business."

"The whole community of Lone Wolf is supposed to show up for the barn raising at the Parlette farm tomorrow morning," Joe said. "While you're talking to Bixby, Phil can warn the man at the bank, and I can go fishing for information."

Having agreed on a plan, the Hardys said good night to Phil and retired to their sleeping bags. Though the floor was hard and the equipment storage room was crowded and dusty, they slept as well as if they were sleeping in feather beds in a royal palace.

By the time Joe arrived at the Parlette farm at seven in the morning, thirty people were already hard at work.

"We assemble the new walls on the ground," Snowdon said as he walked over. He handed Joe a hammer. "Then we raise up the walls and secure them in place."

"I'm sorry about your grandfather being arrested," Joe said.

Snowdon nodded as he cast his eyes toward the ground. "And I'm sorry if I wasn't completely truthful with you. I was trying to protect my grandfather. He thinks he's been set up." Snowdon shook his head and looked at Joe. "I don't know what to believe."

"We're going to do everything we can to find out the truth," Joe assured him. "You can help by telling me everything you know about Toby Gill."

"He seemed like a nice guy to me the few times I met him," Snowdon replied. "Jed McPlat might know more." Snowdon pointed to a young man with red hair and freckles. "He's one of Greg Glover's people. Gill settled a claim for Jed when he totaled his minivan while chasing an F three tornado through a mall parking lot last summer."

Joe walked over and kneeled down to work beside Jed McPlat.

"Joe Hardy's the name," Joe said.

"Howdy," McPlat replied, preparing to secure a slat of wood to the frame.

Joe held the slat steady while McPlat drove in a nail. "Did you hear about Toby Gill disappearing?" Joe asked.

McPlat's next swing of the hammer missed the mark. "No."

"Sheriff San Dimas is concerned," Joe continued. "A lot of people bought tornado insurance from him."

"That's too bad," McPlat said. "Toby's a solid man. I got some good, cheap auto insurance through him."

"And it was legitimate?" Joe asked.

McPlat closed his left eye and peered at Joe with his right. "Yeah, it was legitimate. I wrecked my minivan, and a week later, he gave me the money to fix it."

"Do you remember what insurance company your check was from?" Joe asked.

"There was no check," McPlat said. "I told you, Toby gave me the money to fix it. It was cash."

"Cash?" Joe repeated. No one pays out insurance claims in cash, he thought. Unless they have something to hide, he concluded.

"That is shocking information," Bixby said. He leaned back in his leather chair and shook his head. Frank was seated on the other side of his desk.

"Sheriff San Dimas is probably out at the farm right now, looking for proof in the remains," Frank said. "Even if our hunch about Kanner is wrong, it's not going to hurt anything to delay paying him for a week."

"No, you're right," Bixby agreed. "When you're dealing with such large sums of money, it pays to be prudent. United Insurers has a special team that investigates suspicious claims. I'll have them get right on it."

Bixby shook Frank's hand and walked him to the door.

"Oh, by the way," Frank said, "we don't think Hal Kanner was even at his farm when the storm passed through. He said he called you right after the tornado went through, but I noticed his phone lines were down."

"True," Bixby said, "but he has a cellular phone."

"How do you know?" Joe said quickly.

"I . . . because he used it once when he was in my office," Bixby replied. He opened the door to his waiting room, which Joe noticed was packed.

"Where can I find you if I need to talk to you?" Bixby asked.

"We'll be at the Parlette farm, helping with the barn raising," Frank replied.

Outside Bixby's office building, Frank found Phil waiting to pick him up. "The president of the bank wasn't too keen on delaying the purchase of Kanner's farm," Phil said. "Kanner's selling it dirt cheap, and he's afraid Kanner will just find another buyer."

"I had better luck with Mr. Bixby," Frank told his friend. "He's sending a team of insurance investigators to the Kanner farm. And as long as he withholds that insurance check, Kanner's going to have to stick around."

When Frank and Phil arrived at the Parlette farm, they found Joe red-faced and dripping with sweat, helping to hoist up the first wall of the new barn. "Next time," Joe said, grunting, "I'll go to the air-conditioned office, and you can do the barn raising."

When the wall was in place, Joe took a break, and the two brothers filled each other in on what they had discovered.

"Why would Gill pay Jed with cash?" Phil wondered.

"Maybe he didn't want any record of it," Frank said.

"Or he didn't want Jed to know where the payment came from," Joe added. "I think we need to take a closer look at Gill's insurance office and see how he was running his business."

"And maybe Phil and I can try to track down Hal Kanner," Frank said.

"I don't think we'll have to," Phil said. "He's coming this way, and he looks like he's on the warpath."

Joe and Frank turned to see Hal Kanner moving toward them. "You have a lot of nerve badmouthing me all over town!" he yelled.

People began to move in around them to see what the row was about.

"What's the problem here, Mr. Kanner?" Snowdon asked.

"These kids have been telling the bank not to buy my property," Kanner said.

"Why are you in such a hurry to sell it?" Joe countered. "So that you can leave town before anyone finds you out?"

"Well, boy, maybe if a tornado had destroyed your home and everything you treasured, you'd understand why I want to leave!" Kanner shot back.

"Everything you treasured?" Joe said angrily. "You mean your phony Ming vase and forged paintings?"

"I have papers proving they're all authentic," Kanner insisted.

"I'm sure that's all part of your scam," Joe went on. "You've probably been planning it for months."

Frank put a hand on his brother's arm. "Cool it, Joe."

"Joe, think about what you're saying," Snowdon warned. "How could Mr. Kanner know in advance that a twister was going to destroy his house? It's impossible."

The crowd murmured. "Snowdon's right," one man said.

"Who are these kids? Does anyone know them?" another asked.

Frank could see that they were losing credibility. "We were only trying to clear up a few questions."

"Like how I could call my insurance company if my lines had been torn down?" Kanner asked. He pulled something out of his pocket and held it up for them to see. "Ever hear of a cellular phone?"

"I guess we were wrong, Mr. Kanner," Frank said. "I'm sorry if we've upset you."

Joe turned to his brother, unable to believe his ears. "He could have bought that phone five minutes ago!"

"Chill out, Joe," Frank said sharply, then turned to Kanner. "Please accept our apology,

Mr. Kanner. If you've come to help rebuild the Parlettes' barn, you're obviously not in a hurry to leave Lone Wolf."

"I—I—" Kanner stammered. "I am here to help, that's right."

"Well, then, let's get back to it," Snowdon said. The crowd broke up and returned to work.

Joe was still fuming when Frank pulled him aside. "I think Kanner is guilty, Joe. But we've got some holes in the mystery we have to fill before we go after him."

"So your polite apology was just an act?" Joe asked.

Frank nodded. "Now we've got Kanner stuck here building a barn. The longer we can stall him, the better."

"Don't worry, Joe," Phil said. "Mr. Bixby is sending a team of insurance investigators to Kanner's farm. We'll nail him sooner or later."

"I wouldn't bet on Bixby sending anyone," Frank remarked.

"What do you mean?" Phil asked.

"How did Kanner know we had accused him of lying about phoning Bixby from his farm after the twister hit?" Frank asked. "The only person I've mentioned it to is Bixby, and thirty minutes later Kanner shows up here brandishing a cellular phone."

"So Bixby and Kanner are in this together," Joe said.

"It's possible," Frank replied.

Frank noticed a man with curly black hair and a black mustache who had been edging closer and closer to them while measuring a support beam. He kept turning his ear toward them, as if trying to catch the conversation.

Frank lowered his voice. "But Snowdon had a good point. Even if Bixby and Kanner are working together, how could they predict a tornado?"

Frank thought hard, recalling everything he had seen at the site of the Kanner place—the strange markings on the toppled trees and telephone poles, and the debris patterns that even an expert like Lemar Jansen couldn't explain. "What if there never was a twister?" he said slowly.

"What?" Phil asked.

"What if Kanner was somehow able to recreate tornado damage by some other means?" Frank said.

"It would take the mystery out of the mystery twister," Joe pointed out.

"And give us a motive for why someone jammed radar transmissions," Phil added. "No one would be able to verify that the tornado ever existed."

"Joe, could you and Phil give me a hand moving this support beam?" Snowdon called. Phil and Joe moved to help, and Frank turned to see if the black-haired man was still trying to listen in. The man was nowhere to be seen.

Joe heard a loud creaking noise. From his viewpoint, he could see the ropes that were holding up one of the new walls begin to give way. He realized his brother was right beneath the wall.

"Frank, get out of the way! The ropes are breaking!" he screamed.

Frank looked up just as one of the ropes snapped. The two-story barn wall was about to fall down on top of him!

# 9 The Black-Haired Man

Frank knew he couldn't run beyond the height or width of the great wall before it crashed to the ground. Thinking fast, he took one long stride left and tried to time his leap so that his body would end up in the space left open for the loft's door frame.

"Frank!" Joe screamed again as the wall crashed to the ground with a thundering boom, sending a cloud of dust shooting in every direction.

Joe ran through the cloud, desperate to free his brother from the heavy wooden structure. Joe lifted with all his might, but it wouldn't budge. "Help me get my brother out from under here!" he shouted to the onlookers.

"Forget it," a voice from the midst of the dust cloud said. "I'm over here." Standing in the open door frame, unhurt, was Frank Hardy. Coughing up some dust, he said casually, "Don't try this trick at home, folks."

The Hardys found Phil examining the ropes that had broken. "See how this part is frayed and the other half is smooth?" he said, pointing to the end of the rope. "Someone cut it halfway through."

All the workers had rushed over to help. Joe noticed one person was missing, though. "Where's Hal Kanner?" he said.

"Someone else is gone, too," Frank told Joe. "I saw a man with black hair and a mustache listening to our conversation. He disappeared right before the wall fell."

"There's thirty of us, and we ought to be able to find them," Snowdon said, urging the group in every direction.

Instead of rushing off with the others, Joe paused and scanned the area. He noticed a place in the cornfield where stalks had been trampled down. "Frank, over this way!" Joe called after his brother, then set off at a dead run into the field.

Joe looked both ways down each row as he crossed them. He was crossing his ninth row of corn when someone leaped out from behind and tackled him to the ground. Joe got a glimpse of his assailant out of the corner of his eye before the man ground Joe's face into the red dirt of the cornfield, making it nearly impossible for him to breathe. Joe wriggled and bucked and tried every move he knew, but he could not shake off his opponent. He reached back and got a hold on the man's hair.

"Joe!" he heard his brother shouting from a distance.

At the sound of Frank's voice, Joe's assailant bolted. But his hair did not go with him. Joe rolled over and found he was clutching a curly black wig. He could hear his attacker brushing past stalks of corn and jumped to his feet to pursue the man.

This time he was on his guard when he broke through each new row, but he did not catch sight of the mystery man. He stopped to listen again and heard the sound of machinery being started up. He ran toward the sound and was just able to see the top of a farm machine over the cornstalks. As he drew near, a row of corn in front of him was flattened and cut to shreds by the rotating blade of a giant thresher.

Joe stopped short and began to backpedal, barely able to avoid the churning blades as they grazed his clothing. He stumbled, fell to the ground, and rolled away through to the next row of corn. He made it to his feet just as that row was obliterated by the thresher.

Joe knew he could outrun the machine if he could stay on his feet, but as he crashed through the next row of corn, his path was blocked by a tractor parked there. Joe was trapped with no time to think.

At the last second, he dove beneath the tractor. The blades of the thresher struck the heavy metal frame of the tractor, shooting sparks against Joe's back. His brain was filled with the earsplitting sound of metal on metal. The rotating blades stuck fast, unable to move, and the thresher's engine stalled out.

Joe breathed a huge sigh of relief.

"Joe?" he heard Frank calling again, much closer now.

"Over here!" Joe called back.

Frank and Phil quickly found Joe and helped him to his feet.

"Are you all right?" Phil asked.

"Better than I might have been," Joe joked, pointing to the mangled blades of the thresher.

"What's in your hand?" Frank asked.

Joe looked down and was surprised to see that through that whole ordeal he had not let go of the black wig. "It belongs to the guy who nearly made a pancake out of you and a sausage out of me."

"Did he look familiar?" Phil asked.

Joe searched his memory. "Yes! The morning we got here. It was the man who was driving that unmarked white truck really fast!"

"He would have had to make a quick change somewhere near the barn," Frank said, "but it's possible it was Hal Kanner in disguise."

Snowdon and the other barn raisers helped the Hardys scour the fields for nearly an hour, but there was no sign of either the mystery man or Hal Kanner.

When they returned from the cornfield, Lemar Jansen was waiting. "Phil," Jansen said, "we have to get down to Channel Nine."

"What's up?" Phil asked.

"All morning, Terry Clark has been hyping an interview with Greg Glover that Channel Nine is broadcasting live in thirty-five minutes," Jansen explained.

Just then Sheriff San Dimas pulled up in his squad car. Hal Kanner emerged from the backseat.

"Congratulations, Sheriff!" Joe called as San Dimas got out of the driver's seat. "You found the culprit."

"On the contrary, Joe. Mr. Kanner found me," San Dimas said in a serious tone. "He's lodged a complaint against you and your brother for slander and for threatening him in public."

"If you'll come with us to the Kanner farm, we think we can prove that Mr. Kanner did not lose the priceless artwork he's claiming," Frank said, "and that he faked this mystery twister altogether."

90

"Frank, listen," Jansen said. "The mystery twister *does* exist. That's what the hubbub at Channel Nine is about.

"Greg Glover has videotaped footage of the mystery twister destroying Mr. Kanner's home!"

# 10 Caught on Tape

The TV studio was crowded and buzzing with people when Frank and Joe made their way in with Lemar Jansen and the rest of his Windstormer team. Terry Clark was seated on a small platform in front of the cameras. Seated across from her was Greg Glover.

"I'm extremely doubtful about Greg Glover's presentation since you boys told me about all the things you discovered at the Kanner farm," Jansen said.

A technician signaled for Jansen to be quiet. The broadcast was about to start.

"Good afternoon. I'm Terry Clark with a Channel Nine News extra," the newscaster began. "Today science is one step closer to understanding a rare phenomenon, which meteorologist Greg Glover has dubbed the mystery twister."

Phil and Joe looked at Frank, shaking their heads. "He even stole your name!" Phil said angrily.

"Tell us what we're about to see, Professor Glover," Terry asked him.

"*Professor* Glover?" Jansen scoffed under his breath. "He must have bought off the TV station."

"This is an amateur photographer's video-tape of the event," Glover explained as images appeared on monitors around the studio, including one right over Frank's head.

Frank watched as a funnel cloud dipped down and made contact with the earth. It moved toward the Kanner farmhouse, uprooted trees, and then destroyed the front wall.

"Now watch closely. It will appear to stall for a moment," Glover said. Sure enough, the funnel cloud dissipated and a moment later re-formed. Only now, Frank realized, it was rotating in the opposite direction.

"Notice the clockwise rotation now," Glover instructed. There were gasps from people in the studio. "This is almost unheard of in the Northern Hemisphere and never as part of the same thunderhead that produced a normal tornado."

Frank stared at the screen, dumbfounded, as the re-formed twister, rotating clockwise, demolished the rest of the Kanner house, dropping debris to the right of its path before disappearing once and for all.

The tape was so real, so seamless, Frank began to believe the mystery twister really did exist.

"And who took this footage?" Terry Clark asked.

"The man wishes to remain anonymous for personal reasons," Glover replied. "Although he will make himself known in two days' time."

"You said you had discovered evidence of one other such twister in your illustrious career," Terry Clark said.

"Yes, in New Mexico about five years ago," Glover replied. "But those observations were based on debris patterns. This is the first solid evidence we've had."

"Astonishing," the newswoman said to Glover, then looked into the camera.

"It's a fake!" Jansen exclaimed from the back of the room. The crowd murmured as Jansen made his way up onto the stage. "No force on earth could make a tornado behave like that, and you know it, Greg."

"I know that over the centuries, mankind has claimed hundreds of things to be impossible that we have since proven possible. The mystery twister is the newest of these."

"Let me analyze that videotape if you're so certain," Jansen challenged.

"Currently, I have only the original copy, which has been placed in my hands for safekeeping," Glover explained. "The owner is seeking legal counsel before proceeding with the duplication and sale of the material. In the meantime, I myself will continue to analyze and study the tape at Glover Laboratories."

"Why, you snake oil salesman!" Jansen fumed. Joe saw Terry Clark signal two stagehands to remove Jansen. He beat them to the stage to save the scientist any embarrassment.

"Mr. Jansen, I think we'd better continue this discussion off-camera," Joe said quietly. Jansen scowled at Glover, then reluctantly left the stage.

Outside, the boys convened with Jansen and his team on the Windstormers' red bus.

"I'm surprised the newspeople believed it," Joe said.

"Terry Clark will go to any length to get a sensational story," Jansen told him.

"But would Greg Glover stoop so low as to create a fake tape?" Frank wondered.

"If it meant he would beat me to it and grab the headlines, I think he just might," Jansen said.

"Could the anonymous photographer be Kanner himself?" Phil guessed.

"That's what I was thinking," Frank replied.

"Do you think it's a doctored tape, Phil?" Joe asked their technologically gifted friend.

"Possibly," Phil replied. "But for it to look that convincing, someone must have been up all night working with state-of-the-art equipment."

"Where would someone find equipment like that around here?" Frank wondered.

"Oklahoma Tech," Diana said. "They have a multimillion-dollar computer center."

"If you could supply me with some tornado footage and get me into the Tech computer center," Phil said, "I could see if I can re-create what they did on the tape."

"No problem," Diana said. "I have a student pass."

"And I've got a library full of tornado videos," Jansen added. "The big storm front we're waiting for has stalled in the Gulf of Mexico, so we won't have any weather until at least this evening."

"Great. Why don't you, Phil, and Diana head over to Oklahoma Tech?" Joe suggested to Frank.

"Where are you going, Joe?" Frank asked.

"To jail. I want to talk with Henry Low River again. I also want to see what Sheriff San Dimas has found out about the owner of that black wig," Joe replied.

"We'll meet up at Windstormer headquarters at three o'clock," Frank said. The others agreed, and everyone trooped off the red bus, heading in two directions, eager to begin investigating.

"Framed, baby!" Henry Low River muttered, pacing in his cell in the Lone Wolf jail. "Someone's nailing my hide to the wall."

Joe nodded. He felt bad for the man. "Have they found the body?"

"What body? There's no body," Low River railed. "Gill is alive."

"Deputy Klement said they pulled a forty-five-caliber slug out of Gill's car seat," Joe said.

"But I didn't fire it!" Low River insisted.

"The lab report said your Colt revolver had been recently fired," Joe replied.

"I wasn't even at my house yesterday afternoon," Low River explained. "I was hunting for deadwood in the forest. Someone slipped into my house, took my gun, shot Gill's car, and put the gun back."

"What about the knife Snowdon found in Gill's office?" Joe asked.

"Planted there. I didn't even know I was missing it until Snowdon brought it to me last night," Low River told Joe.

Joe raised an eyebrow. "So you're saying someone broke into your house *twice* to take things—without your noticing?"

"They wouldn't have to break in," Low River moaned. "I don't lock my doors."

Joe studied the man's face, looking for any telltale signs of deceit. In spite of what the sheriff thought about Henry Low River, Joe firmly believed the man was telling the truth.

"And you're certain Gill is the same man who ripped you off in Texas?" Joe asked.

"I'll never forget Todd Allan Miller's voice," Low River said in a low tone, nodding. "That's what Gill called himself then."

"And when you followed him around the back of the truck stop that morning, he disappeared?" Joe asked, reviewing the story. "Did you notice anything unusual?"

"Nope," Low River responded. "Just trucks."

Joe rose from his chair. "I'll find out what I can," he said.

Joe walked down Main Street, trying to make sense of the string of strange occurrences that seemed to him unusual for a small town. He looked across the way at Gill's insurance office. The front door was still marked off with bright yellow police tape.

Joe knew he was breaking the law, but he had to get another look inside Gill's office. Finding a window ajar, Joe opened it, then climbed inside. He could see that all the surfaces had been dusted for fingerprints, but many of the articles in the room were still in place. He was looking for something—anything—that might give away Gill's true identity or shed light on his sudden disappearance.

The insurance policies Gill had written were all gone, but in the bottom drawer of the filing cabinet, Joe found one blank form and read the letterhead: "K-State Insurers, Kansas City, Missouri."

The name struck Joe as familiar, but he could not remember where he had seen it before.

The framed photo of Toby Gill caught Joe's eye. The smiling man with the upturned nose, blond and balding, looked so sincere and honest. Then Joe noticed something on his shelf in the background of the photograph. The penholder that had been found wedged against the gas pedal of his car! Odd, Joe thought, that a kidnapper would think to grab something off his victim's shelf to use to drive his car into a river eight hours later. He decided to borrow the picture to show Frank and Phil.

The drawers of Gill's desk were filled with appraisals of customers' homes and businesses but nothing of interest. Stuck behind the top left drawer, Joe found a check for $450 from Andrew Parlette made out to Tamco. Joe figured Andrew Parlette must be Snowdon's father. The memo on the check read: "Six-month tornado insurance premium."

Joe knew that a premium was the payment a customer had to make to an insurance company.

Why is the check made out to Tamco if the parent insurance company is K-State Insurers? Joe thought. It suddenly struck him where he had seen the name before. He double-checked. On the office wall, he found the Certificate of Excellence awarded to Toby Gill by K-State Insurers.

If anyone knows about Toby Gill, it would be them, Joe reasoned. Picking up the phone, he found it was still working and dialed the phone number listed on the form.

"K-State Insurers," a man's voice said.

99

"Yes, hello," Joe said. "I was just curious whether you have a salesman named Toby Gill working for you?"

"Yes, we do," the man answered.

Joe dropped his shoulders and sighed. Toby Gill was for real.

"Can I help you?" the man asked.

Joe thought quickly. "I was calling to let you know he's been missing for the last two days."

The man on the phone laughed. "No, he isn't. I know exactly where he is."

"Where?" Joe asked, stunned.

The man laughed again. "Toby Gill is sitting right next to me!"

# 11 Uncovering the Impostor

"That's impossible," Joe said into the phone.

A second man with a deep, robust voice spoke to Joe. "This is Toby Gill. What can I do for ya?"

Joe explained who he was and where he was and what had happened, concluding with the question, "How did someone in Lone Wolf, Oklahoma, assume your identity, Mr. Gill?"

Gill thought for a moment. "About three years ago, an arson fire gutted our office building. I thought that certificate and all those official insurance documents had been burnt up, but it sounds like the same fella that started the fire stole all my papers!"

"Weren't you suspicious about the claims you had to pay out to customers in Lone Wolf?" Joe wondered.

101

"We never paid out anything. We never even processed any forms from Lone Wolf, Oklahoma," the real Gill insisted.

"I'll let the local sheriff know about this— pronto," Joe assured him. "Oh, by the way, are you connected to a company called Tamco?"

"Tamco? Never heard of it," the real Toby Gill replied.

"Tamco?" Deputy Klement repeated the name Joe had asked about and leaned back in the sheriff's leather desk chair. "Sure, that's a subsidiary of K-State Insurers. I write my checks for my car insurance to them."

"K-State Insurers has never heard of Tamco," Joe told Klement, showing him the check from Andrew Parlette. "My guess is Tamco is Toby Gill, or, rather, his impostor."

"But Toby's made good on a couple of claims this year," Klement argued. "Jed McPlat, for one."

"He paid Jed in cash, probably out of the money he had collected from his other customers," Joe guessed.

"And you're saying Henry didn't kidnap Gill, or whoever he is?" Klement asked.

"Right," Joe replied. "The impostor collected as much in insurance premiums as he could. But he knew once tornado season came, he was going to have to start paying out big time. He knew you would suspect Mr. Low River, so he framed him to throw us off the track while he escaped."

"Probably on the other side of the world by now," Klement remarked. "Say, Henry, where'd you see this fella last?" Klement called down the hallway to the jail cells.

"Behind the Dust Bowl, where they park the trucks," Henry's voice called back.

"The trucks," Joe said to himself as something dawned on him. He began connecting the dots, linking the events of the last two days. "The impostor isn't on the other side of the world. He's still in Lone Wolf!"

Frank checked his watch. Phil had been at work in room 136 of the Oklahoma Tech Computer Center for nearly three hours. Finally, the door opened. "Come on in," Phil told Frank and Diana.

Frank stood over Phil's shoulder while his friend cued up the tape he had created. "By editing together various tornado footage and using computer imaging to delete, enhance, or otherwise manipulate certain static background elements, I've created a five-point-nine-second tape."

"Huh?" Diana asked.

"Would you like me to expound?" Phil asked, turning his swivel chair toward her, delighted.

"No, Phil, we don't have time," Frank warned.

"In three hours, you've created five point nine seconds?"

"And I rushed," Phil said. "There are numerous imperfections. If Glover created the tape we saw this morning, it would have taken him all night to do it."

Phil pressed the Play button. The image on the screen was of two grain silos beneath a dark thunderhead, with a partially formed funnel cloud behind them. The tornado touched down, tore apart the first silo, stalled for a moment, then began rotating in the opposite direction, continuing to move forward and hit the second silo.

"That's it," Phil said, pausing the tape. "Five point nine seconds."

"But enough to prove that the mystery twister tape could have been doctored," Frank said, patting Phil on the shoulder. "Good work."

As Frank, Phil, and Diana were passing the sign-in desk at the computer center, Frank stopped to talk with the student on duty. "Excuse me, who was at this desk last night?"

The student looked to Diana, uncertain whether to answer.

"It's okay, Erin, he's a friend of mine," Diana assured her.

"Actually," Erin replied, "I was here. The other guy who does this was sick."

"Can I have a look at the sign-in sheet from last night?" Frank asked. He skimmed through the names, but none of them seemed familiar. "And you checked all their student ID cards?"

"I always do," Erin answered.

"Was there anyone in the computer center last night whom you didn't recognize?" Frank asked as he handed her back the roster.

"No," Erin replied. "Wait. Yes! The new janitor."

"What did he look like?" Frank asked.

"He was tall," Erin replied, casting her eyes at the ceiling as she thought. "He had a mustache and black curly hair."

"The mystery man who attacked Joe!" Phil exclaimed.

"We now know more about what he's been up to," Frank said. "But we still don't know *who* he is."

Frank, Phil, and Diana left the computer center and headed across campus to the student parking lot.

"What now?" Diana asked.

"If we can prove Glover's tape is a fake, then we'll have Kanner," Frank replied.

"That's easy," Phil said. "Give me thirty minutes in the computer center with that videotape, and I can tell you whether or not it's been doctored."

"That means we'd have to sneak into Glover Laboratories and take the tape from right under his nose," Frank pointed out.

"Right," Phil replied.

"You call that easy?" Frank asked.

"Glover has been trying to hire me away from Jansen for months," Diana said. "And I'm friends with Jed McPlat. I could at least get us in the door."

"Sounds good. We'll take Diana's Jeep," Frank said. "Meanwhile, Phil can take the Blue Bomber to Windstormer headquarters and let Joe know the game plan. We'll all meet back here at the computer center at five o'clock. Hopefully, with the mystery twister tape in hand."

"Wait!" Phil said, grabbing Frank by the shoulder. "What about Bixby?"

"What do you mean?" Frank asked.

"If your hunch is right about Bixby, and he's working with Kanner, he's going to get United Insurers to issue that check for one point seven million dollars *today*," Phil reminded Frank. "By the time we prove they're crooks, they may be long gone."

Frank crossed his arms and leaned back against Diana's Jeep, thinking. After spotting a pay phone outside the school cafeteria, he hurried to it and dialed information.

"Could I have the number for the main office of United Insurers?" Frank asked the operator.

"What are you doing?" Phil asked as he and Diana caught up to Frank.

"Thank you, operator," Frank said into the phone. He hung up and dialed another number,

106

covering the mouthpiece with his hand. "Remember when the cassette deck got stolen out of the van? The insurance guy was going to reimburse us. Then Iola Morton said she thought that cassette deck had been sold to her brother, Chet."

"Yeah, but she didn't know that Chet had backed out of the deal," Phil reminded Frank.

"But because of Iola's one comment, the insurance company made us get all this verification before they would pay Joe and me the four hundred dollars back," Frank explained, then removed his hand from the mouthpiece to speak. "Hi, United Insurers? I can't identify myself, but the tornado damage claim for one point seven million dollars on the Kanner farm in Tulip, Oklahoma, is a fraud."

Frank hung up the phone.

"But we aren't *sure* it's a fraud," Phil says.

"No. And if it's for real, Kanner will eventually get his money. But if United Insurers lets Mr. Bixby hand over that payment to Mr. Kanner *this afternoon*, I will eat the hat of every cowboy in Oklahoma," Frank said, joining the others in laughter.

"Dad? It's me," Joe said over the telephone in Jansen's office. "Sorry to call you collect again, but I need a favor."

"All right, Joe, shoot," Fenton Hardy said.

Joe explained as much as he could about the

insurance fraud, impersonation, and other scams he believed were being committed in Lone Wolf. "I need some information, and it's the kind of information only you can get for me."

Fenton Hardy didn't speak for a moment. They both knew what Joe was asking. Mr. Hardy was a one-time police officer and now a private investigator. Over the years, Frank and Joe had come to believe their dad had some link to every branch of law enforcement in the country.

"Do you need me to use my contacts to get information from police files or government files?" Mr. Hardy asked.

Joe cleared his throat. "Both. I need everything you can get me about a company called Tamco and an insurance salesman named Alvin Bixby and an art collector named Hal Kanner."

"Pertaining to . . . ?" Fenton asked.

"Insurance. Claims, fraud, background, anything," Joe said.

Fenton chuckled. "Is that all?"

"Um, no! One more thing," Joe said. "Anything you can dig up on a man named Todd Allan Miller. That may be an alias."

"Is he the president of Tamco?" Fenton asked.

"Maybe," Joe said, furrowing his eyebrows, puzzled. "What made you ask?"

"Todd Allan Miller. T.A.M.," Fenton explained. "His corporate abbreviation would be—"

"Tamco!" Joe jumped in. "Dad, you're a genius. Thanks!"

Joe gave his father the number at Windstormer headquarters so he could call back with his findings. Outside Jansen's office, Joe ran into Phil.

"Boy, do I have news for you," Phil told Joe.

"You can tell me on the way to the Dust Bowl Truck Stop," Joe said, turning Phil right back around and out the door.

"What's at the Dust Bowl?" Phil wondered as he hopped into the driver's seat of the Blue Bomber.

"I have a hunch about the man in the black wig," Joe replied, "and I want to prove it."

Frank pushed through the revolving door of the new office building that was home to Glover Laboratories.

"Nice place, huh?" Diana asked. "Glover has corporate sponsors, so his facilities are a bit more deluxe."

"Why doesn't Mr. Jansen get corporate sponsors?" Frank asked as they stepped onto the elevator.

"He doesn't want anyone pressuring him or telling him what to do," Diana explained. "Why, Frank? You want to switch camps?"

Frank smiled. "What? And give up the dog kennel?"

109

The elevator stopped on the sixth floor and opened into a reception area for Glover Laboratories. Behind the receptionist's desk were large tinted windows that looked in on what Frank guessed was Glover's control room. Radar screens, high-tech graphic computers, and various atmospheric monitors lined the wall, manned by half a dozen technicians.

"It looks like Glover could have doctored that videotape right here," Frank said quietly to Diana as they approached the receptionist.

When they reached the desk, Diana said, "Hi, I'm Diana Lucas."

"Yes, I know," the receptionist replied coolly.

"Would you let Mr. Glover know I'm here?" Diana continued. "I'd like to talk to him about that job he's been offering me."

"Mr. Glover isn't available," the receptionist replied. "If you'd like, you can make an appointment for next week."

Jed McPlat stepped out of the lab into the reception area, holding a file folder. "We need this delivered to Terry Clark at Channel Nine," he told the receptionist.

"Hi, Jed," Diana said with a warm smile.

Frank saw Jed's face light up when he saw her. "Diana! What are you doing here?" he asked.

"I wanted to talk to Mr. Glover about a job," Diana replied.

"You told me you would never work for him," Jed reminded her. "What changed your mind?"

110

"Oh, well . . ." Diana began.

Frank saw she was at a loss for words and jumped in. "The mystery twister tape is going to bring Glover Laboratories national recognition and a lot more funding. We want to be a part of that."

Jed gave Frank a sour look. "Mr. Glover's analyzing the tape right now. Diana, you're welcome to come in, but your friend has to wait here."

Diana looked to Frank, who nodded that it was all right. While the receptionist was buzzing in Jed and Diana, Frank slipped up to the control room window to get a better look. He could see Glover looking at a video monitor, and he recognized the image of the so-called mystery twister tearing apart Kanner's home. Glover appeared to be watching the tape frame by frame, rewinding, and watching the same section again.

"Excuse me. You'll have to wait downstairs," the receptionist said sharply, and rose from her desk to escort Frank out.

Standing in front of the office tower, Frank wondered why Glover would be studying his own videotape. Maybe trying to fix any glitches that could prove it had been fabricated, he thought.

A small object suddenly struck Frank on the back of the neck and fell to the ground. Frank scooped the object off the ground. It was an earring.

Looking up and blocking the sun from his eyes,

111

Frank was able to see someone waving to him from an upper-floor window. It was Diana! Without warning, she threw something else out the window.

Frank watched the object fall two floors before realizing it was black and rectangular. It was the videocassette!

Frank bolted toward the building. But the tape was falling faster than he was running. If it hit the concrete, their key piece of evidence would be broken into a hundred pieces!

# 12 A Spectacular Theft

Diving and stretching like a football receiver, Frank nabbed the tape just before it hit the ground, then landed on the concrete with a thud.

A businessman walked past Frank, who was laid out on his stomach near the front step, and gave Frank an odd look.

"How are you?" Frank gasped from the ground, giving the man a friendly wave with the videocassette. Frank groaned as he rose to his knees, feeling his ribs. Those will be black and blue by tomorrow, he thought to himself.

He looked up, trying to find Diana in the sixth-story window.

"Here I am!" Diana called, speeding out the revolving door. "I tripped a circuit breaker, and while they were trying to restore power, I snagged the tape,'' she explained as they raced to the Jeep.

"How did you get away to find the main electrics box?" Frank asked.

"They think I'm fixing my makeup in the bathroom," Diana said, grabbing the roll bar and swinging into the driver's seat.

"Nice work, Diana," Frank said, looking at the videocassette. "Now the rest is up to Phil."

"A cream-colored sedan? Nope, never saw it," the short-order cook at the Dust Bowl Truck Stop told Joe and Phil.

"Did you see this man?" Phil asked, showing him the photo of the Gill impostor. "We think his name is Todd Allan Miller."

"No. Sorry, boys," the cook replied. "I see a hundred different guys a day."

"We should get moving, Joe," Phil said, turning to leave. "We're due to meet your brother and Diana back at Oklahoma Tech."

Joe got an idea. Taking a black felt-tipped pen from a display on the counter, he drew on the glass plate covering the photo, adding curly black hair and a black mustache.

"What about this man?" he asked the cook.

The cook laughed at first, then stopped. "Hmm. A driver who looked like that parked his truck out back overnight about two days ago."

"An unmarked white truck?" Joe asked.

"I think so," the cook said.

"Thanks," Joe said, smiling with excitement. "Come on, Phil."

"Okay, I admit it," Phil said as they left the truck stop, "I'm confused."

"Picture this," Joe said, leading Phil around the building. "Henry Low River follows our Gill impostor from his office to here. What's the only way a car and a man could suddenly disappear at a truck stop?"

Phil looked around him. "If he drove his car into the back of a truck!"

"Right. Our impostor then puts on his disguise and becomes . . ." Joe waited for Phil to fill in the blank.

"The mystery man!" Phil exclaimed, grinning.

"One and the same," Joe pointed out. "We passed his truck on our way in from the airport."

"Right," Phil said. "He was headed for Tulip."

"And for Hal Kanner's farm, is my guess," Joe went on. "Remember the tracks Frank found? They were made by an eighteen-wheeler."

"But why would Hal Kanner need a truck?" Phil asked. "What was on it?"

Joe snapped his fingers. "Once I was visiting a friend's farm, and his dad had to tear a stump out of the ground. He wrapped chains around it and uprooted it with his tractor."

"And Frank saw tractor tire prints at Kanner's farm!" Phil exclaimed.

"My guess is they used a tractor and some other equipment they had in the truck to tear

Kanner's house down and then claim it was a tornado that did it."

"So Gill—I mean, this Miller character—is Kanner's accomplice?" Phil asked.

"That's my hunch," Joe said. As he opened the passenger door of the Blue Bomber, he stopped dead and stared past the corner of the truck stop café. "Phil, it's there."

Parked among a dozen other tractor-trailers in the back lot, Joe saw the white, unmarked truck.

"Come on, Phil," Joe said, walking toward the back lot.

"Wait. What if Miller's here?" Phil asked, not moving.

"After nearly dropping a barn on Frank and running me over with a thresher," Joe replied, smacking the palm of his hand with his fist, "I kind of hope he is here."

Joe crept cautiously up to the cab of the white truck. Jumping up on the running board, he looked inside the cab. No one was there. "Let's check around the back," he told Phil, who had reluctantly joined the search.

Rounding the back of the trailer, Joe saw that the rear door was sealed and apparently locked

"It's hydraulic," Phil explained, examining the door closely. "Lowers outward from the top, see, creating a loading platform. Or, if you lower it all the way to the ground . . ."

Phil let Joe fill in the blank this time. "A ramp," Joe concluded. "Can we open it?"

"No controls on the outside, so they must be in the cab," Phil replied.

"And being the mechanical wizard you are, you probably can devise a way to get to it," Joe said, smiling.

"Yes, using a complex, technologically advanced technique," Phil joked. "Find me a coat hanger."

Five minutes later Phil slid a coat hanger between the driver's window and the door, hooked the locking mechanism, and pulled it up.

Phil and Joe climbed in and began searching for the controls to the rear door.

"Hmm," Joe muttered as he picked up a black metallic device from under the passenger seat. "I wonder what this is."

"I can tell you exactly what that is," Phil said, taking the device from Joe and looking it over. "It's called a black box. They're standard Air Force issue on fighter jets."

"You mean a black box as in 'flight recorder'?" Joe asked.

"No, I mean black box as in 'radar jammer,'" Phil replied.

"Now we know how they pulled that off," Joe said, searching the dashboard for the controls to the rear door. "Here!"

"Yup, those are the controls," Phil confirmed.

"Stay here and keep an eye out, Phil," Joe instructed as he hopped down from the cab.

Phil nodded and pressed a button. Joe watched

117

the rear door slowly lower until it was parallel to the ground. Joe jumped up onto the loading platform and walked into the trailer.

The compartment was filled with machinery, a huge tractor with an electric winch and a set of chains, hooks, and pulleys attached to the back. That must be what left the marks on the trees at Kanner's farm, Joe thought. Under a tarp, Joe found a wood chipper and a snowblower, which he guessed were used to splinter pieces of the house and to spread dirt, broken glass, and other debris after the tractor had pulled down the walls.

Opening a large chest, Joe found a chain saw, a nail driver, and a pile driver. "Your basic portable tornado," Joe said quietly to himself. Circling around to the other side of the compartment, Joe found a wooden crate near the door.

Removing the top with a pry bar from the tool chest, he discovered it was filled with heavily wrapped and padded objects. Opening the first package, he gasped. It was a vase with the same pattern as the fragment he had found on the farm.

Tearing away some paper covering a framed portrait, Joe quickly recognized the image of the Pilgrim. Joe was not an art expert, but he had a strong hunch he was looking at two genuine artifacts. Kanner had purchased the real items so that he could insure them to the hilt, Joe guessed, and then destroyed cheap copies.

Joe returned the pry bar to the tool chest. Hearing voices outside the truck, he ducked down behind the wood chipper. He recognized the first voice as Hal Kanner's. "See anyone in there?"

"No," the other man replied. Joe wondered why Phil hadn't warned him. Maybe he had slipped away to get help.

"Help me load this on," Kanner said.

Joe heard the two men groan as they hefted something onto the back of the truck. Joe peeked around the wood chipper. An oblong object wrapped in a plastic tarp had been loaded into the truck.

"No way you can push that check through?" Kanner asked.

"United Insurers put a stop-payment order on it, so no bank will give us cash for it," the other man said. "And United won't let me issue you another check until there's a complete investigation."

"I'll bet money it's because of those nosy kids," Kanner snarled.

"Let's cut bait and clear out," the other man ordered. "Empty the Tamco account and head south for the border."

"Give up one point seven million dollars?" Kanner griped. "Are you crazy, Alvin?"

Alvin, Joe thought. It's Alvin Bixby!

"I'd rather have the half million from Tamco

and be a free man than be a millionaire in prison," Bixby argued. "Grab that crate. We'll put it in my car."

"What about the equipment?" Kanner asked.

"We can't save it this time," Bixby replied. "I'll follow you out to the Brafford Quarry. We'll send the truck and the whole shebang over the edge and into the basin."

Joe heard the two men dragging the crate with the Ming vase and painting off the back of the truck. A chance to escape, he thought.

Moving cautiously from his hiding spot, Joe was alarmed to hear the hydraulic door being activated. It was closing.

Joe rushed forward and was about to leap through the opening when he heard a moan. It was coming from inside the plastic tarp.

"Phil?" Joe called.

"Yeah," his friend answered groggily.

Joe knew he couldn't pull Phil out in time. He refused to leave his friend behind.

Joe watched as the rear door closed with an echoing bang, throwing them into darkness.

# 13 The Telltale Weather Vane

Frank pressed the Stop button on the editing machine in room 136 at the Oklahoma Tech Computer Center.

Diana sighed loudly. "Do you want to watch it again?"

"How many times will this be?" Frank asked.

"Number twenty-five," Diana replied.

"Phil would know exactly what to look for," Frank lamented, checking his watch. "It's five-thirty. Where are they?"

"Wherever Phil and Joe are, I'll bet they're having more fun than we are," Diana remarked. "Frank, we're in a lot of trouble. If we can't prove this is a fake, Glover can have us arrested for stealing it."

Frank nodded and gave a sigh. "We might as

well keep running the tape until they get here," he suggested. "Glover kept watching the same two seconds of tape over and over again."

Frank found the spot in the mystery twister tape, and he and Diana watched it frame by frame.

"Something's not quite right," Frank remarked.

"What do you mean?" Diana asked.

"My brain knows something's wrong with this picture, but my eye can't find it," Frank replied, backing up the tape frame by frame. "That's it!" he exclaimed.

"What?" Diana asked.

Frank pointed to a tiny object on the screen. It was on the roof of the Kanner farmhouse, barely visible.

"The weather vane?" Diana wondered.

"Keep your eye on it while I run this section again," Frank told her.

Frank pressed Play. The mystery twister hit the side of the house, tearing away one wall. It stalled a moment, then rotated in a clockwise direction. Frank paused the tape.

"It never moved!" Diana exclaimed.

"Bingo!" Frank said. "Two-hundred-mile-an-hour winds spinning in two different directions, and the weather vane never moved."

"We got 'em!" Diana shouted, giving Frank a high five.

"Now my biggest concern is Phil and Joe," Frank said.

"Maybe they're just running late," Diana offered.

"Joe knows better," Frank told her. "In detective work, *late* means *trouble*. Let's check back at Windstormer headquarters, see if they've heard anything."

"Then we'd better get Sheriff San Dimas this videotape," Diana added.

Frank was surprised to see Greg Glover's monster truck and San Dimas's squad car parked in front of Windstormer headquarters. "Looks like we're having a party," Frank tried to joke.

"Have you heard from my brother or—" Frank began to ask, walking into Jansen's office.

"Look who's here," Glover huffed. He and San Dimas were standing beside Jansen.

"Did you steal the twister tape from Mr. Glover?" Jansen asked.

"Yes, we did," Frank admitted. "And we apologize."

"That's not good enough." Glover sneered.

"Neither is this," Frank replied, holding up the video cassette. "It's a fake."

Frank ran the tape on a VCR in the Windstormer control room, pointing out the telltale weather vane that never moved. All eyes fell on Glover.

"I guess it's my turn to apologize," Glover

said, bowing his head. "I shouldn't have accepted the authenticity of the tape so quickly."

"Are you saying you didn't create it yourself?" Diana challenged.

"No, I did not. It was brought to Glover Laboratories by a man with curly black hair and a mustache," Glover explained.

"The mystery man," Frank said.

"Not anymore," San Dimas said. "The lab in Tulsa found strands of blond hair in the black wig."

"Kanner had brown hair," Diana said, shaking her head, disappointed.

"But Toby Gill was blond!" Frank said, recalling the photo they had seen in his office.

"This strand of hair wasn't just blond, it was *dyed* blond, with brown roots," San Dimas explained. "I cut Toby Gill's hair once, and I remember—he had blond hair but brown roots."

"So it was Toby Gill who created the fake tape and gave it to Mr. Glover," Frank deduced.

"Only he used the name Miller," Glover told them.

"Sounds like a man of many faces," Jansen said.

"And names," Frank added. "Miller is the name of the man who swindled Henry Low River."

"I've dropped all charges against Henry," San Dimas told Frank. "He's gone home with his grandson."

"Good," Jansen said. "Maybe now we can get back to the business of chasing tornadoes."

"Not yet," Frank said. "Phil and my brother are missing."

The phone in the control room rang. "This could be them now," Jansen said as he lifted the receiver. "Hello? . . . No, but Frank is."

Jansen offered Frank the phone.

"Is it them?" Frank asked.

"It's your father," Jansen replied.

Frank slowly put the receiver to his ear. "Dad?"

Frank listened as Fenton Hardy covered all the facts he had dug up at Joe's request. "Five years ago Hal Kanner received two hundred twenty thousand dollars in an insurance payment on a collection of Tiffany lamps he lost in a tornado in New Mexico."

"New Mexico?" Frank repeated, then covered the phone to tell Jansen. "I think I've solved the riddle of the first mystery twister."

"The insurance company was Southwest Home and Auto, and the representative handling the case was—"

"Alvin Bixby?" Frank guessed.

"On the nose, son," Fenton said. "We came up empty on the name Todd Allan Miller, but judging by the details of the scams Joe described, my colleague in Dallas said it sounded like a lifetime con man whose real name is Dutch Wise. He changes names like a jockey changes shirts and

125

has been involved in insurance and real estate scams from Missouri to Texas."

"Sounds like our man, Dad," Frank told him.

"And tell Joe that Tamco is the name of a dummy company in Lone Wolf," Mr. Hardy added. "In short, it's a post office box and a bank account."

"I would like to tell Joe that," Frank replied. "But right now we don't know where Joe is."

Joe banged his fist on the rear door of the truck, hoping someone might hear him. But the metal door was thick and solid, and Joe figured the highway noise outside would drown out any sound he could make.

Phil was sitting up, recovering from the blow to the head Kanner had dealt him after sneaking up on him in the cab of the truck. He held a penlight, illuminating the trailer slightly.

"Sorry, Joe," Phil said. "Next time maybe you should be the lookout."

Joe smiled, covering his concern that there might not be a next time for Phil and him. Joe felt the truck shudder, and the ride got bumpy. "We're off the main highway, Phil. Maybe even on a dirt road," Joe reported. "Can you work any Phil Cohen magic on this door?"

Phil shook his head. "The hydraulic cables run under the truck. Basically, we need a battering ram."

Joe looked at the nose and grille of the huge tractor. "Have you ever hot-wired a tractor?" Joe asked.

"No," Phil replied with a half-smile. "But I'm willing to try."

Joe held the penlight while Phil went to work. Using a number of different tools from the chest, Phil soon had the ignition switch dismantled and rewired.

"Cross your fingers, Joe," Phil said as he touched two wires together. With a sputter and a bang, the tractor engine came to life.

Joe slapped his friend on the back, then hopped into the driver's seat. Putting the tractor in gear, he gave it full throttle. The nose of the tractor crashed against the heavy rear door with a thundering sound.

Joe backed up, and Phil moved in to check the progress. "Barely dented it."

"I need a running start," Joe realized. Jumping off the tractor, he and Phil began moving the snowblower, wood chipper, and other cargo to the side.

Joe backed the tractor up an extra twenty feet, then put it in gear and floored. The nose of the tractor hit the door with such impact, sunlight flashed through a crack in the top before the door bounced back into place.

"Get it up, Joe!" Phil cheered on his friend.

Joe rammed the door again and again. On the fifth try, the door gave way slightly.

"We've breached the integrity of the seal!" Phil shouted.

"What?" Joe asked.

"We've cracked the door open!" Phil clarified.

Joe saw that he needed to open the crack about another six inches in order for him and Phil to squeeze out.

Suddenly, the truck came to a stop. Joe feared that at any moment Kanner would be putting another rock on the gas pedal to send the tractor-trailer into the Brafford Quarry.

Joe backed up the tractor as far as he could, crushing the wood chipper as he backed over it. Giving it the gas one last time, Joe rammed the door with the nose of the tractor, separating it from the frame by several more inches.

Phil stuck a leg through the opening, then squeezed his body through. "Come on, Joe!" he called, standing on the rear bumper.

Joe jumped down from the tractor. The truck lurched forward, knocking him off his feet.

"Hurry!" Phil shouted.

"Go!" Joe shouted at his friend. Instead, Phil reached back through the opening, helping Joe up.

The front of the truck dipped violently. Joe squeezed through the crack, but it was too late.

The back of the truck had cleared the quarry's edge and was plummeting through space with Phil and Joe clinging to it for dear life!

# 14 A Hundred-Foot Drop

Joe watched the sheer cliff of the quarry passing by in a blur. Forcing himself to look down, he saw the surface of the water coming up fast. If they stayed glued to the truck, Joe knew they would be crushed against it when it hit. "Push off!" he yelled to Phil.

Fighting the G-forces, Phil and Joe pushed away from the truck, landing hard in the water a safe distance away from the twenty-ton vehicle. The impact of the landing stunned him, and he could see a wall of water explode around the truck.

Joe fought to stay conscious, searching the surface of the water for his friend. Phil was floating facedown about fifteen feet away. Putting Phil's chin into the crook of his arm, Joe swam toward the side of the quarry, looking for a place to get out.

The walls of the quarry were sheer rock that rose straight up out of the water. Finding no shore or rock face to climb up onto, Joe hung on to a small jut in the cliff face and floated in the water.

Phil coughed up a mouthful of water. He was still stunned by the impact, but at least he was conscious.

"How are you doing, buddy?" Joe said.

"I've been better," Phil answered, managing a weak smile.

Scanning the hundred-foot-high rock wall that surrounded them, Joe realized they would never be able to climb out on their own.

"What's the plan, *amigo?*" Phil asked, grabbing on to the same jutting rock as Joe.

"Think good thoughts," Joe told his friend. "And hope that we're rescued."

"This is an all-points bulletin." Frank spoke into the CB radio in Diana's Jeep. "We are still on the lookout for a light blue 1973 pickup truck, being driven by two males in their late teens."

"Frank, it's Greg Glover. Still no luck. I'm going to check out Alvin Bixby's office."

"Thanks, Mr. Glover. Over and out," Frank replied. He put the CB microphone in its cradle with a sigh. He and Diana had been up and down every street in Lone Wolf but had seen no sign of Joe or Phil.

"Where would they have gone?" Frank wondered aloud.

"Do you want to head over to Tulip?" Diana asked.

"Good idea," Frank replied. "We can take a look at the Kanner farm on the way."

Riding down the highway toward Tulip as the sun began to set, Frank spoke aloud to help him think. "Let's say I'm Joe. I find out Toby Gill is an impostor. I want to find the impostor. What do I do?"

Frank's train of thought was broken when he spotted the Parlette mailbox at the end of the dirt drive leading to their farm. "Pull in here," Frank told Diana. "Maybe Snowdon knows something."

Frank and Diana found Snowdon and his grandfather sitting on the farmhouse porch with Bullet, the hound dog. Snowdon was laughing over a story Mr. Low River was telling him. When Frank approached and explained that Joe was missing, the two men grew serious.

"I owe Joe big-time," Low River said. He told Frank about his last conversation with Joe. "When I mentioned how Gill—or, rather, Miller—disappeared behind the truck stop, Joe took off like a rocket."

"The truck stop—of course!" Frank shouted. "Come on, Diana."

131

"I know the owner of the Dust Bowl," Snowdon said. "I'll call ahead."

Frank paced nervously while Snowdon spoke on the phone with his friend at the Dust Bowl.

"Light blue, uh-huh," Snowdon said. "It's there?" Snowdon gave Frank the thumbs-up sign. "Oh, you haven't?"

Frank could tell by Snowdon's tone that something was wrong.

Snowdon thanked his friend and hung up. "The blue pickup is there," Snowdon told Frank, "but no one's seen Phil or your brother since about four-thirty this afternoon."

Franked checked his watch. It was nearly 7:00 P.M.

Joe looked up at the cloudy, starless night sky, framed by the dark edges of the Brafford Quarry. Sometime, long ago, Joe thought, slate or granite had been mined there. Over the years the bottom of the quarry had gradually filled with rainwater.

Joe winced. His attempts to keep his mind off the pain and weakness he felt in his arms were not working. After three hours in the water, he and Phil were waterlogged and as wrinkled as prunes. "Got any more jokes, Phil?"

"None that I have the strength to tell," Phil replied.

Joe heard distant thunder, then another sound. He pricked up his ears. "Listen."

132

The two could hear a distant, mournful howl. "Unless it's Lassie, I doubt that a dog's going to be able to save us."

"The sound is getting closer," Joe said. "And it sounds pretty frantic, too."

"Slow down, Bullet," a voice echoed from above.

"Phil, it's Bullet!" Joe exclaimed.

"Who?" Phil asked.

"Snowdon's dog!" Joe shouted. "Hello!" he called. "We're down here!"

A few minutes later, a flashlight tied to the end of a long rope was lowered to Joe. Joe knew Phil was in worse shape than he was, so he tied the rope around his friend's waist.

"Ready!" Joe shouted. "Pull him up!"

Joe watched as Phil ascended, rappelling like a mountain climber off the edge of the quarry as he was pulled up and out of sight.

Finally, the rope reappeared, and Joe tied it around his own waist. Every inch of his body ached from the bumps, scrapes, cold, and fatigue he had endured. He started up.

"Joe, it's Henry Low River!" a voice called down. "Listen, if this rope breaks, you need to—"

"Forget it!" Joe interrupted with a shout. "If this rope breaks, I quit!"

Joe heard laughter from above and couldn't help but smile himself. When he reached the top, Frank grabbed his arm and pulled him over the edge to safety.

"Joe!" Frank exclaimed, hugging his brother.

"Are you okay?" Diana asked.

Joe nodded, smiling.

"Here we are hot on the trail of three criminals, and you and Phil are off taking a swim," Frank joked, setting everyone laughing again.

Wrapped in blankets and riding in the back of Snowdon's pickup, Joe and Phil listened as Frank and Mr. Low River explained how they had tracked them to the quarry.

"The owner of the Dust Bowl had seen the white truck leave and head north on the highway," Frank continued.

"So with Snowdon and me in the pickup and Frank and Diana in the Jeep, we began hopscotching exits," Low River said, picking up the story. "Then finally, at the seventh exit, the guy at the taco stand remembered seeing the truck."

"Mr. Low River is the one who spotted the tire tracks where Kanner had pulled off the paved road," Frank explained.

"It's that Cherokee blood," Low River said, grinning. "We're excellent trackers."

"We used a sock we found stuffed under the seat of the Blue Bomber to give Bullet the scent, and he used his nose to find the owner," Frank said, pointing to Phil.

"Just think—if not for my messy nature and

smelly feet, we might still be down there," Phil said with a laugh.

At the Dust Bowl Truck Stop, Frank, Joe, and Phil hopped out of Snowdon's truck just as the skies opened up. Diana, who had followed Snowdon from the quarry, pulled up beside them.

"See you back in town!" Low River called as he got into the cab of Snowdon's pickup.

Frank saw Diana scrambling to throw a tarp over her Jeep.

"Why don't you leave it here for tonight?" Frank suggested while he helped Diana batten down the tarp. "You can ride back with us."

Frank, Joe, Phil, and Diana all managed to squeeze into the cab of the Blue Bomber. Phil turned the key, and the engine started right up. "Hey, on the first try," he noted. "Maybe our luck is changing."

Heading back down the highway toward Lone Wolf in the heavy rain, Frank and Joe filled each other in.

"So Bixby, Kanner, and Miller were working together," Joe concluded, "setting up in one area, pulling off insurance scams, and then moving on and starting again."

"That's my guess," Frank replied. "Bixby would just get a job with a new insurance company, Kanner would buy another home out in the country, and Miller would arrive later, starting a low-cost insurance business to *compete* with Bixby."

"Congratulations, guys," Diana said. "I think you've finally put an end to their crime spree."

"Yeah, the only problem is, they're probably halfway to Mexico by now," Joe said.

Frank saw Phil's eyes start to close. "Phil!" he shouted.

Phil jerked his head up. "Sorry, Frank. I don't think I've been this exhausted in my life."

"Ten minutes and you'll be in bed, old buddy," Joe said, patting his friend on the shoulder.

Phil hit the brakes suddenly, throwing Joe forward so that he clunked his head on the windshield. The Blue Bomber fishtailed and came to a halt less than a foot away from Sheriff San Dimas's squad car.

"Can I say two things?" Joe asked, touching a fresh bump on his head. "Number one: ouch. Number two: I'm driving."

Frank saw that the side door of the squad car was caved in and the rear tire was badly twisted. "Looks like the sheriff's been in an accident."

Frank and Joe got out to see if anyone needed help. Frank put his hand to the windshield of the squad car and peered in. "No one inside!" he yelled to Joe through the driving rain.

Joe looked along the side of the road to see if anyone had been thrown from the vehicle. "No one here, either!" he yelled back. Just then, he nearly stumbled over a twisted cylinder about three feet long. Picking it up and seeing the red and white spiral stripes, he realized it was a barber's pole.

"I don't get it, Frank!" he yelled. "It's from San Dimas's barbershop, but we're still five miles away from Lone Wolf!"

Frank thought for a moment. His heart jumped. Running back to the Blue Bomber, he reached over Diana and turned on the radio.

". . . has devastated the town of Lone Wolf," the radio news broadcast was saying. "Once again, our breaking story, a tornado believed to be an F four or F five has touched down in Lone Wolf, Oklahoma, and is moving northwest. . . ."

The transmission was interrupted by static interference.

"An F five is the most powerful tornado we know of," Diana said. "It can have wind speeds of three hundred miles an hour."

"You mean the tornado lifted up the sheriff's car and dropped it five miles away?" Joe asked.

"With an F five, it could happen," Diana said.

"The question is," Frank added, "where is the tornado now?"

The four of them stopped and listened as the wind howled around them. Joe was looking off to the left when five cloud-to-ground lightning bolts struck at once, illuminating a tornado funnel more than a mile wide.

"There it is!" Joe shouted. "Looks like it's about five miles north of us. Just wait until the lightning strikes again."

Everyone peered into the rainy night. Thirty seconds later lightning lit up the sky. Joe thought the funnel looked even bigger.

"It's shifting," Diana told them. "The tornado's coming back this way. It's headed right for us. We've got to get out of here—fast!"

# 15 Monster Truck Terror

"Let's get moving, Phil!" Joe shouted. He hopped into the driver's seat and squeezed in so he could close the door to the cab.

Joe turned the key in the ignition. The engine started for a split second, then cut out. He tried again.

"I thought you just needed to jiggle it right!" Frank shouted to Phil.

Phil reached over and tried the ignition switch three more times. With each try, the sound got weaker and weaker. "Sorry, guys. The alternator's dead."

"We might all be joining the alternator if we don't think of something fast," Joe said grimly. "The tornado's getting closer."

Frank spotted headlights coming their way.

Jumping into the middle of the road, he waved frantically. The pickup truck came to a stop, and the driver stepped out. "Snowdon!" Frank cried out.

"An overpass has crashed down onto the highway. We can't get to Lone Wolf!" Snowdon shouted.

"Our car is kaput—useless," Frank told him.

"Pile in," Snowdon said, waving the others out of the Blue Bomber.

A jackrabbit raced across the highway. Bullet jumped out of Snowdon's pickup and ran off into the night after it.

"Bullet!" Snowdon shouted.

"I'll get him," Joe said.

"Bullet will be okay," Snowdon said. "We need to think about ourselves right now."

Snowdon's pickup had two jumper seats in the back. Still, when Joe pulled the door closed behind him, he felt like a sardine.

"Turn on the CB, Joe, and tune in channel nineteen," Diana instructed from the backseat. "Let's see if the Windstormers are out there."

"Mayday, mayday, this is Joe Hardy!" Joe said into the microphone.

"Mayday?" Phil wondered. "That's the distress call for airplanes."

"And we might be airborne any second now," Joe replied, watching the massive whirlwind advancing toward them.

"Joe, this is Lemar Jansen," Jansen's voice came in over the CB. "I'm telling you, you don't want to be chasing this monster."

"That's affirmative, Mr. Jansen. *We don't,*" Joe radioed back.

"The Windstormers have detailed road maps and radar on the bus," Phil said. "Maybe Mr. Jansen can tell us the best way to avoid it."

"What is your exact location now?" Jansen asked.

Joe handed the microphone to Henry Low River, who gave Jansen a detailed description of their surroundings.

"You should be coming up on a dirt road on your left. It's C-two-one-one-nine. Take that," Jansen instructed.

"I see it," Snowdon said, turning left off the highway. "I'm much obliged."

"I'm much obliged, too," another voice chimed in on the same frequency. "I see exactly where they are."

"Who was that?" Frank asked.

"I know that voice," Low River said. "It's Toby Gill."

Joe cupped his hands and looked out the window on the passenger side. Greg Glover's monster truck was a second away from broadsiding them.

"Look out!" Joe shouted.

The massive black truck hit Snowdon's pickup just past the passenger compartment, sending it rolling down an embankment into an irrigation ditch.

When the truck came to a stop, Joe found himself lying on top of his fellow passengers. The truck was on its side, and water from the ditch was flowing in through the broken driver's-seat window. Joe could see that Snowdon and Low River were groggy and groaning. Diana appeared to have been knocked unconscious.

Frank was pinned beneath Phil. He could feel a hard metallic object jabbing him in the back. "Your window is the only way out, Joe!" he yelled to his brother.

Joe tried to roll down his window, but it stuck fast. "The door was smashed in when we rolled," Joe said. "It won't open!"

Frank removed the object that was jabbing him. "It's a tire iron!" he yelled, handing it to Phil, who passed it on to Joe.

Joe swung the iron bar, striking the shatter-proof glass with enough force to crack the entire surface of the window. He kicked the glass out with his foot and climbed out onto the door.

Joe saw the F5 twister only a few hundred yards away, a column of black that tore up the earth as it went. He spotted a small plane flying upside down around its perimeter. He realized the F5 must have passed by the local airport— and that the aircraft had no pilot.

"Give me a hand, Joe," Frank shouted.

Joe tossed the tire iron up onto the bank and

pulled Frank through the window. "We've got to hurry!" he shouted, pointing to the F5, which had reached a water tower about a hundred yards away.

"Get in the ditch," Frank said, "and help them get to solid ground as I pull them out."

Frank took Diana from Phil. He pulled her through the window, then lowered her down to Joe. Joe waded through three feet of water, carried her up the bank of the ditch, and gently put her down.

Joe saw headlights approaching. Glover's monster truck was zeroing in on him. Spotting the tire iron on the ground, Joe grabbed it and charged the oncoming vehicle.

After leaping high into the air, Joe landed on the hood and rolled into the windshield. Clinging to a wiper blade with his left hand, Joe swung the tire iron into the driver's-side window with his right hand, cracking it.

Joe's second blow crashed through the window and made contact with the driver. The monster truck spun to the right and down into the irrigation ditch, throwing Joe off the hood. The giant left front wheel trampled over Snowdon's pickup, barely missing the passenger window where Frank and Phil were lifting out Low River and Snowdon.

Joe jumped to his feet and swung himself up onto the runner of the monster truck, ready to knock Glover out of commission.

Lying across the seat, knocked cold by the first blow from the tire iron, Joe saw the Toby Gill impostor, Dutch Wise.

Frank heard the creak of metal giving way and watched in horror as the water tank was torn from the top of the tower and thrown against the ground. A flood of water rushed down the irrigation ditch, stranding Frank, Phil, and Snowdon on top of the pickup.

Frank saw a greater danger. The roaring column of the F5 was approaching a telephone pole. As it snapped the electrical cables, sparks flew from the live wires. If they touched the water, Frank knew thousands of volts of electricity would be conducted through the liquid and into the metal frame of the truck he and his friends were trapped on.

The tornado winds broke the telephone pole in half. "The wires!" Frank screamed as the pole with its live electrical cables fell toward the ditch.

# 16 Caught Inside a Tornado

Seeing the mammoth tractor tires that kept the metal body of Glover's truck high over the water line, Frank got an idea. "Jump on the tires!" he shouted to the others. He remembered that rubber did not conduct electricity.

Phil, Low River, and Snowdon jumped onto the front left tire, while Frank vaulted over the hood and landed on the front right tire, just as the cables hit the water upstream, sending a powerful electric current coursing through Snowdon's abandoned vehicle.

"Good thinking, Frank!" Phil shouted.

"You saved our bacon from being fried to a crisp!" Low River added.

"Our bacon's not saved yet. Everybody into

Glover's truck!" Joe yelled over the din from the F5 which was now bearing down on them.

Joe saw that Frank was shouting something back, but the roar of the wind made him feel as if he were inside a jumbo jet engine. He couldn't hear a word his brother was saying.

Frank leaped off the tire and onto the bank. Once Phil, Low River, and Snowdon were inside, Joe threw the truck into reverse. The three-inch treads of the monster truck tires grabbed the solid ground beneath the mud in the ditch and propelled them up the bank.

Frank was waiting, bracing himself and Diana against the gale.

Joe recoiled as the windshield was shattered by the immense pressure of the tornado winds. As Phil pulled Diana into the cab, Frank felt his feet being lifted off the ground. He clutched the door handle with all his might.

Joe felt the rear tires of the truck break contact with the earth. Frank wasn't inside, but Joe knew he had no choice. He floored it.

Joe felt like a fish struggling on the end of a hook as the force of the mighty truck battled against the force of the tornado.

Frank's body was suspended in midair, and his grip on the door handle was slipping.

Joe threw the truck into low gear. The front tires grabbed hold and pulled them forward. The rear end dropped down and got traction.

Joe sped across the open field with Frank riding on the runner and holding on for dear life. The deafening roar lessened.

"You can stop, Joe!" Frank shouted. Joe either didn't hear him or wasn't listening. "You can stop!" Frank yelled at the top of his lungs.

Joe brought the truck to a halt.

"It's gone," Frank said, taking a deep breath. "It's over."

Joe and the others turned around and looked. The F5 had dissipated, leaving only the ravaged countryside behind to remind them that it had ever been there.

Dawn had taken forever to come, Frank thought. Even though they were exhausted, the Hardys couldn't sleep. The first light brought hope, but it also brought the harsh reality that the town of Lone Wolf was in shambles.

Frank walked out of Windstormer headquarters and realized it was one of the few buildings left standing.

"Good morning, Sheriff," Joe greeted San Dimas, who was unlocking Jansen's office.

"Morning, Joe," San Dimas replied.

"How's the prisoner?" Joe asked. He looked through the door at Dutch Wise, who had been handcuffed to Jansen's desk for the night.

"I think the prisoner is wishing he had never heard of Joe Hardy," San Dimas said, smiling.

"I'm just sorry the other two got away," Joe said.

"I wouldn't be so sure that they did," San Dimas said. "It would have been nearly impossible to get out of this area last night."

"I would have gotten out," Dutch Wise grumbled, "if it wasn't for these lousy kids."

Deputy Klement pulled in front of Windstormer headquarters and let out Greg Glover. "Mr. Glover!" Frank shouted when he saw the squad car.

"Sorry, Frank," Glover said. "I went looking for Bixby at his office last night and found Dutch Wise. I hear my truck caused you a lot of trouble."

"It also saved our lives," Frank told him.

Joe came out of the building with San Dimas and the others.

"I've got good news and bad news, Sheriff," Klement told San Dimas. "The good news is I found your squad car."

The Hardys, Phil, and Diana couldn't help laughing, well aware of the news to come.

"Look who made it home," Low River said, pointing down Main Street. Bullet was running full tilt, howling all the way. The dog jumped up onto Snowdon and licked his face.

"Bullet found his way back to Snowdon," Low River said. "He must be part Cherokee."

Snowdon laughed. "I think he's part cat, and he's used up about eight of his nine lives."

"Deputy Klement," San Dimas said, "why don't you give Mr. Wise here a ride to the jail in Tulsa, since our jailhouse doesn't have a roof anymore."

"My pleasure," Klement replied.

"I was sure we would have been able to nab Bixby and Kanner," Frank said.

"Sheriff San Dimas thinks they may still be in the area," Joe told him, "though I don't know how we would find them in this mess."

Frank thought a moment, then looked at Snowdon's dog. "Bullet!"

"What about him?" Phil asked.

Frank pulled Alvin Bixby's business card from his wallet. "It's a long shot, but maybe Bullet can pick up Bixby's scent."

Snowdon let his dog sniff the card, then said, "Now go git 'im, boy."

Bullet walked over to Frank first. "Not him! Find Bixby!" Snowdon commanded, and let Bullet sniff the card again.

Bullet took off, with Frank, Joe, and the others following closely. The hound dog roamed one direction, then the next, sniffing the ground, until Joe figured they had covered half the square footage of Lone Wolf.

Finally, outside Alvin Bixby's office, Bullet picked up a scent and led Frank and the group to another one of the few buildings in town that the tornado had left untouched.

"The bank," Frank said, exchanging a look with Joe. Where else would two greedy crooks like Bixby and Kanner go?

Joe, Frank, and Phil entered the bank, accompanied by Sheriff San Dimas.

"That's the bank president," Phil told them, pointing to a man in a suit, seated across a desk from two other men in baseball caps and sunglasses.

"There you are, gentlemen," Frank could hear the bank president telling the two men. "The balance of the Tamco Corporation's account."

"I'll take that," San Dimas said, grabbing the suitcase with one hand and pulling out his revolver with the other. Kanner and Bixby looked up, stunned to find themselves surrounded by the Hardys and citizens of Lone Wolf.

"There are a lot of insurance policies that need to be paid off with that," Joe said, grinning at his friends.

Three days later the Hardys were packed and ready to go home to Bayport. Kanner, Bixby, and Wise were in jail, and the town of Lone Wolf was well on its way to rebuilding.

"Can I give you a ride to the airport?" Phil asked.

"To tell you the truth," Frank replied, "we've decided to take a train."

"That's a pretty long trip. Why would you want to take a train home?" Phil asked.

"After our week in Twister Alley," Joe said with a laugh, "we don't want our feet to leave the ground for a long, long time."

# THE HARDY BOYS® SERIES  By Franklin W. Dixon

## LOOK FOR AN EXCITING NEW
## HARDY BOYS MYSTERY COMING FROM
## MINSTREL® BOOKS